BATTLE RIVER PRAIRIE

A Journey of the Heart

DJ ATKINSON

I

Copyright © 2024 DJ Atkinson

All rights reserved

Some of the characters and events portrayed in this book are based on real people and situations. Most parts have been fictionalized in varying degrees, for various purposes. All of the dialogue is purely fictional. This is a work of fiction. Names, characters, places, and incidents either are the product of the author's imagination or are used fictitiously.

No part of this book may be reproduced, or stored in a retrieval system, or transmitted in any form or by any means, electronic, mechanical, photocopying, recording, or otherwise, without express written permission of the publisher.

ISBN: 9798878027717
Imprint: Independentley Published

Cover design by: DJ Atkinson
Library of Congress Control Number: 2018675309
Printed in the United States of America

Second Edition July 2025

To Dee Dee for introducing me to her Grandmother

and Tyson for letting me be me.

DJ ATKINSON

CHAPTER 1

Dawn slipped through the muslin drapes not as light, but as liquid gold—thick, deliberate—pooling in the warped seams of the floorboards and spilling over the uneven contours of Mary's room. The air held its breath, dense with the hush of a morning unclaimed. She lay still beneath the covers, one arm stretched across the bed as though reaching for something—or someone—not there. Her eyes remained closed. The dream had already slipped away, but she clung to its shape, reluctant to trade silence for the weight of the day.

Then: a knock. Bright, rhythmic. Cecile. Always on time. Always a little too alive.

"Morning, Miss Mary," came the voice, lacquered in cheer. "It's seven-thirty. Breakfast will be ready shortly."

The curtains drew back with a practiced sweep, letting the gold flood in. It climbed the bedpost, lit the creases of her linen nightdress, and washed her at its insistence. She flinched at the brightness, turning away like a fox in its den, unwilling to be seen just yet.

"Are Mother and Father up?" she asked, voice slow with sleep.

"Mr. Percy's had his breakfast," Cecile replied, already moving through the room like she owned the map. "Out for his walk."

"He didn't wait?" The words emerged as a whisper. No blame, just the quiet sting of being left behind.

Cecile crouched to retrieve the slippers that had slid beneath the bed. She placed them gently at Mary's feet—less housekeeping than benediction. "You know how he is—always chasing the hour."

Mary sighed, a small sound weighted with love and something close to loneliness. The door clicked shut behind Cecile, leaving her alone again in the golden hush.

She touched her jaw, fingers skimming the blunt edge of her haircut. The habit was new—reflexive, defiant. The crop was sharp, decisive. Less a style than a severing. Not rebellion against her family, exactly, but against the world that had prewritten her role in cursive.

Downstairs, the breakfast room waited in its usual arrangement: linen exact, porcelain poised. Mrs. Percy sat like a figure carved from habit, the newspaper unfolded with military precision, her eyes combing the headlines.

"Good morning, Mother."

Her mother looked up. The smile she offered was brief, practiced. "Your father had hoped to show you the blossoms this morning. A shame you missed him."

The comment landed with more weight than its softness suggested. Mary nodded and took her seat, though her thoughts wandered—not to cherry blossoms or footpaths, but to the letter tucked away upstairs.

India.

That damned letter.

She had imagined opening it in a rush of joy, heart quickening, the air around her charged. She had read it twice before the disappointment set in, and a third time to make sure the refusal was real.

The Obstetrics Program: full. Or closed. Or simply not available to her.

The details didn't matter. The dream had been folded away with the letter—quietly, like a garment no longer in season.

Her fingers traced the rim of her teacup. Across the table, her mother turned a page with crisp finality. The world, it seemed, remained indifferent. She took a breath, shallow but steady, and returned her focus to the cup between her hands—white china, fragile, warm.
Julie entered with a fresh pot of coffee. Mary mouthed a soft thank-you, cradling her cup as though it could warm more than her hands.

"You drink far too much coffee, Mary," her mother said, tone clipped, affectionate in its own antiseptic way.

She smiled faintly. "I suppose I do."

The sip burned her tongue. She welcomed the sting. It was sharper than the ache behind her ribs.

Her mind slipped again to what might have been: the smell of spices in the air, the low hum of monsoon heat, the urgent rhythm of learning in a place that would have pushed her to the edge of herself. She'd pictured sun-bleached courtyards, women in labor, the hush before birth and the cry after. She had imagined it all so vividly she could almost believe she had already been there.

But she was here. At the same table. With the same porcelain. In the same life.

The clock struck nine.

She blinked. "I'm late for my shift!"

In one motion, she rose, grabbed a biscuit, drank the last of her coffee—scalding or tepid, she didn't care—brushed her mother's cheek with a kiss, and vanished in a gust of linen and resolve.
"Careful, or you'll trip!" her mother called after her, amusement threading the words. But Mary was already gone.

She ran.

The air bit at her cheeks, and her boots cracked against the frost-rimmed street, each step a punctuation mark in the day's unwritten sentence.

The rejection still pulsed, but it had changed shape—less wound now, more fuel. She would go elsewhere. Learn differently. Cut her own path through the dense thicket of expectation.

She lengthened her stride. The wind caught her coat and pulled it open like wings.

Not lost—becoming.

CHAPTER 2

Mary walked the park's winding path toward Birmingham Children's Hospital, her steps unhurried, her spirit buoyed by the hush of spring's awakening. The gravel crunched softly beneath her shoes, a counterpoint to the quiet symphony of birdsong overhead and the rustle of early leaves. Around her, the world opened like a secret finally shared—daffodils nodding in golden clusters, sunlight unfurling in splinters through budding trees, and the sweet tang of soil rising from flowerbeds, rich with promise.

She paused at a curve in the path, drawn toward a patch of wild blossoms. Their delicate faces turned upward, they seemed to hum with secrets only the earth could keep. She knelt, brushing her fingers lightly over a petal. Its cool softness stirred something in her—a kind of yearning she could not yet name. For all the ambition she carried, all the carefully laid plans, moments like this reminded her that some parts of life were meant to be felt, not charted.

Then—chaos.

A sudden chorus of whirring wheels and bright shouts broke through the calm. A bicycle club, all legs and laughter, swept past like a summer storm. She staggered back, her heel catching on the uneven path. In an instant, she tumbled into the flowerbed, a flurry of skirts, soil, and startled breath.

For a beat, she lay there, dazed—half in shock, half in disbelief. The scent of earth was stronger at this level: raw, grounding. Grass clung to her hem, and a smear of dirt streaked her sleeve. But even before she rose, laughter welled up from somewhere deep within. Low and unrestrained, it escaped her like the sudden flight of a bird.

"Well," she murmured, brushing herself off, "the park demands its toll."

Grass-stained and wind-kissed, she gathered herself, not with embarrassment but with a grin that widened as she walked on. It was a small humiliation, yes—but a delightful one. The kind that reminded her not to take herself too seriously. The kind that stitched her back into the world with humor and grace.

At the park's edge, the pastoral hush gave way to Birmingham's vibrant sprawl. Carriages rattled by, streetcars groaned, motors spewed past, and pedestrians darted in practiced choreography. The city pulsed with its usual urgency, pulling her into its orbit. She pressed forward, thoughts shifting to the hospital, her pace quickening with purpose.

In the quiet of the doctors' cloakroom, she stood before the small wall mirror, dabbing at the grass stain on her skirt with a damp cloth. The worst of it remained—stubborn, green, and unmistakable—but at least the dirt had been coaxed away.

She adjusted her collar, smoothed her hair with the heel of her hand, and reached for her white coat hanging on the peg beside hers. Slipping it on felt like stepping into her second skin—creased in the elbows, the pockets weighty with habit. She buttoned it briskly, her movements economical, practiced.

For a moment, she looked at herself again. A hint of pink still lingered on her cheeks, and a smudge of soil clung near the hem. Let it. The day had begun with earth and laughter—she would carry that with her.

She turned toward the door, the doctor now fully in place, the girl in the park tucked lightly into memory.

Inside, the familiar cadence enveloped her: the click of heels on polished floors, the low hum of conversation, the occasional peal of a child's laughter. The hospital was its own living thing—fragile, resilient, unpredictable. Just like the people within it.

She moved through the corridors with practiced ease, her stained dress drawing a few curious glances she welcomed with a flash of wry amusement. She stepped into a ward where sunlight filtered through high windows, casting long stripes across the beds.

She knelt beside a young girl cradling a worn doll, its stitched eyes barely intact. The child's arm was wrapped in gauze, her expression wary.

"Let's take a look," she said, her voice as soft as gauze itself. She began to unwrap the dressing with gentle fingers. "Healing beautifully—you'll be climbing trees again in no time."

The girl flinched. "Mama says girls shouldn't climb trees. Says we're safer at home."

Mary paused, her expression softening. She glanced at the nurse, then back to the girl.

"Can you keep a secret?" she whispered.

The girl nodded solemnly.

Mary leaned closer. "I climb trees all the time. Fell out of one this morning, in fact."

She rose and parted her coat like a magician revealing a trick. The grass-stained dress beneath spoke volumes. She watched the girl's smile bloom, a ripple of delight she hadn't expected to cause. A flicker of kinship passed between them—mischief shared across generations. The stain, once a mark of clumsiness, now felt almost like a badge. Not shame, but a secret kind of pride. The girl gasped, then giggled —a sound that rose like light. The nurse smiled, shaking her head with quiet admiration.

Mary handed over the soiled gauze. "Fresh dressing, please. And let her parents know she'll be ready to go home soon."

She turned to leave, but paused when the girl called, "Doctor Mary?"

She knelt once more. "Yes, love?"

"Can I tell you a secret?"

She nodded, her tone suddenly reverent. "Of course."

The child leaned in and whispered into her ear, the words too soft for anyone else. Whatever she said, it pulled a rare stillness into Mary's expression, as if the room itself had held its breath.

When she rose, the moment clung to her like the fragrance from the flowers that morning—faint, impossible to forget.

She moved down the corridor, the rhythm of the hospital resuming around her. The laughter of a child, the warmth of shared mischief, the quiet power of being trusted—these were not interruptions in her day. They were the point of it.

And though the morning had begun with a fall, she walked forward now with the quiet certainty of someone who knew that even the stumble was part of the journey.

BATTLE RIVER PRAIRIE

CHAPTER 3

In the Doctor's Lounge—a sanctuary tucked away from the bustle of Birmingham Children's Hospital—Mary found a moment of quiet refuge. The afternoon light filtered through tall windows, spilling across worn armchairs and a heavy oak tea cart, the latter manned by the ever-faithful tea lady. The aroma of biscuits, jam, and steeping Earl Grey hung in the air, familiar and soothing.

Henrietta Atkinson waved her over from a corner table cluttered with books and papers. Only a year or two older than Mary, Henrietta shared more than a profession—she shared the same hunger for purpose, the same restless spark.

Mary navigated the mess with practiced amusement, balancing her cup and plate before sliding into the chair opposite.

"I'm sorry, I've made a complete mess of things," Henrietta said, sweeping a stack of papers aside with a smile.

Mary eased into the seat across from her, setting down her saucer. "How's your day going?"

"Exhausting. I've been on since dawn. Had a birth at five, then ward rounds, then a consult with that fussy neurologist—what's his name with the enormous moustache?"

Mary smiled. "You'll have to narrow it down.

Henrietta snorted. "Fair. Let's just say I'm ready for retirement and I'm only twenty-nine."

Mary glanced at the chaos on the table. "Well, you certainly know how to make yourself at home."

"If you think this is bad, you should see my flat. It looks like someone let loose a librarian during a storm."

Their laughter was a brief reprieve—natural, warm, earned. But as it faded, her gaze drifted. The letter. India. The sound of her mother folding the paper. The sting of a dream shelved.

"Well," she said, "at least you have a placement to go to."

Henrietta paused, confused. "What do you mean? We're out of here in five months. What happened?"

Mary reached into her bag and handed her the letter. Henrietta scanned the lines quickly, her brow furrowing.

"The position I hoped for is unavailable. I need to find something else for this year."
Henrietta looked up. "That's tough. But perhaps it's for the best. Your parents weren't thrilled about India, were they?"

She gave a small nod. "They'll be relieved, I suppose. I'm not."

Henrietta was quiet a moment, then her eyes lit up. She rifled through a stack of journals and tugged one free.

"Here. Canada! They're looking for women doctors in Western Canada. Country work, midwifery experience preferred. Look."

Mary leaned in. The advertisement was plain, but something in its phrasing tugged at her—like a hand extended from across a wide ocean: Strong energetic Medical Women wanted for country work in Western Canada, under the Provincial Government Department of Health.

"Canada?" she repeated.

"Yes," Henrietta said. "It's a change, but maybe a better fit. You'll still be helping women in need. Still delivering babies. Still learning."

She studied the ad, her fingers smoothing the edge of the page. Canada—so far from India, so foreign, so unknown.

"I know so little about it," she admitted.

Henrietta gave her a sly smile. "Which means it's ripe for adventure."

Mary looked up, surprised by how gently the idea had begun to unfurl inside her, like a sapling pressing through frost.

"I'll post an inquiry tonight," she said, half-surprised to hear herself say it aloud.

Henrietta beamed. "That's the spirit."

A few days later, Mary wandered the gardens behind the hospital, the new letter still in her hand. It bore the emblem of Dr. Johnstone and the words Fellowship of the Maple Leaf.

Gone was the sharp sting of India's refusal. In its place, a swelling curiosity.

The children's laughter carried from the hospital steps. A bench beckoned beneath a blooming cherry tree, and she sat, unfolding the letter. It was kind. Encouraging. The position in Northern Alberta was open. They welcomed her application.

She let the paper rest across her knees, its edges fluttering slightly in the breeze. When footsteps approached, she didn't move to hide it.

"What are you reading?" Clara's voice rang out. "We

were calling you from back there. You didn't hear us."

Before she could answer, Clara plucked the letter from her lap with a grin.

Mary retrieved it gently, smoothing a faint crease with her thumb. Then, with a breath, she folded it and slipped it into her satchel beside the other—the Indian dream now softened, quieted. The papers brushed together like two pages in an unfinished chapter, and the bag felt heavier for it.

Henrietta's eyes sparkled. "So you wrote to her! Good. What does it say?"

"I've applied. They want women doctors in Northern Alberta."

Clara blinked. "Alberta? Where in God's name is that?"

"I checked an atlas. It borders the Rocky Mountains."

Henrietta looked delighted. "Rocky Mountain Spotted Fever, Tick Paralysis—it all sounds delightfully exotic."

Clara looked horrified. "Why would they want female doctors? You'll be alone in the wilderness. Bears. Wolves."

Mary raised an eyebrow. "Thank you, Clara. That hadn't occurred to me."

Clara backpedaled. "Just saying..."

Mary grinned. "It's easier for women anyway—we can cook and clean for ourselves."

Henrietta chuckled. "You? Cook? Clean?"

"What are you saying?"

"You can't cook and you don't clean."

Mary conceded. "A temporary drawback."

Henrietta pressed further. "Do you even know how to ride a horse?"

"I haven't since I was ten."

Clara cackled. "You've got more bustle than brawn, Percy. You ought to get more exercise."

Mary rolled her eyes. "You'll train me, I'm sure."

"We'll get you riding, cooking, and lighting fires. You'll be ready for Alberta yet."

She grinned. "I've used Bunsen burners. Close enough?"

Their laughter echoed through the garden.

Her voice softened. "It's a chance to make a real difference. In a place I've never imagined."

Henrietta leaned in, her voice filled with wonder. "The Fellowship of the Maple Leaf. Sounds like a quest."

Clara nodded. "Ask about supplies and conditions. But

go. You must."

Mary looked toward the cherry blossoms, her thoughts a thousand miles away.

India had been a dream. But maybe Canada was calling her to something deeper.

She didn't yet know the shape of it—but it felt like something that could last.

CHAPTER 4

In the heart of bustling Birmingham, within the hallowed walls of Dr. Johnstone's office, the air was thick with the scent of old paper, bergamot tea, and something older still—the unspoken weight of choices made across distant continents. Dr. Emma Johnstone, a woman carved from the bedrock of medicine and war, sat at her desk like a relic from a vanished world. Her eyes, sharp and kindly, belonged to someone who had seen the limits of suffering and chosen to remain kind.

Her office was less a room than a map of memory. Ivory carvings from Calcutta, a sun-bleached ostrich egg from Nairobi, a jagged hunk of quartz from Alberta's Peace River country. On the wall, a cracked but still-glorious map of Canada spread out like a frontier still to be tamed. Mary stood just inside the threshold, the toes of her boots grazed the rug's edge —an invisible line she wasn't yet sure she'd earned the right to cross.

Her eyes caught on a worn brass idol from India, its patina dulled by time and touch. She had once imagined her own brass-slicked future there—rich with spice, smoke, and voices raised in prayer. The beaver pelt mounted nearby seemed to breathe in contrast: colder, wilder, asking something more of her.

Dr. Johnstone rose with a grace that belied her years. "Doctor Percy. Welcome, welcome. Please come in."

Mary stepped forward, heart thudding in a strange rhythm—half excitement, half mourning. Their handshake was firm, charged with possibility. She offered a smile, tempered but earnest. "Doctor Johnstone, it's an honour. I was admiring your collection."

"Ah," Johnstone said, with a wave at the chaos around her, "Yes, well. My house looks worse. These bits are all that made the cut. One day, they'll bury me with a suitcase full of spoons and postage stamps. Come. Tea?"

Mary nodded. They sat. The clink of china. The soft slosh of tea. A prologue to something larger.

"I'm very pleased you're interested in the position. We need every able hand in Canada, particularly in the north. There are places where the nearest doctor is days away. Sometimes more."

Mary folded her hands. "When would the position begin? When would they need me?"

"The Fellowship of the Maple Leaf is offering to pay passage for a group of candidates in June," Johnstone said, stirring sugar into her cup. "It's an Anglican initiative—British aid for British settlements. Church workers, nurses, teachers. Mostly financed by old money."

"I'm Anglican," Mary said simply.

Johnstone's mouth tugged into something between approval and relief. "Good. That will make things easier. The United Farmers Party currently in power in Alberta has... strong opinions. A government doctor cannot be Catholic."

Mary blinked. "Because of politics?"

"Because of politics," Johnstone confirmed. "In Alberta, religion and party lines are stitched tight. You're fortunate—your background fits exactly."

A flicker of unease passed through her. This intersection of faith and opportunity felt precarious. But she said nothing.

"I won't lie to you," Johnstone continued. "It will be hard. You'll be the only physician for miles. You'll deliver babies in snowstorms, treat broken limbs by lamplight, stitch wounds without anaesthetic. You'll be doctor, nurse, sometimes priest."

Mary met her gaze. "I want that. I want to be needed." Johnstone nodded once, as though Mary had passed an invisible test.

"Good. Then here's some advice: before you go, spend a week at the Dental Hospital. Learn to pull teeth. You'll do more of that than you can imagine."

The suggestion landed like a stone dropped into still water. Tooth extraction had never figured in her dreams of medical heroism. And yet—the image rooted: a shivering boy on a cabin floor, a swollen jaw, no help for miles. She nodded.

"Thank you. I will."

Johnstone set down her cup and reached across the desk. Her hand was warm, papery, strong.

"Mary, you couldn't be more perfect for this."

That single sentence pressed itself into her like an anointment. A confirmation. She felt the pull of something vast—not destiny, exactly, but a deep invitation.

The meeting ended with shared smiles and a lingering quiet. Outside, the Birmingham air was cool and grey.

But inside her chest, something sparked and flared.

CHAPTER 5

In the refined district of Birmingham, Mary's footsteps echoed against the cobbled streets, crisp and deliberate. She passed couples in tailored coats, dogs trotting beside them, the whole scene lacquered in aristocratic ease. The scent of coal smoke, lavender, and the faintest trace of wet stone lingered in the air as she approached her family's grand city home. Its wrought-iron gate and manicured garden stood like sentinels of tradition—imposing, pristine, and altogether too orderly for the news she carried.

Inside, Harris, the footman, greeted her with a practiced nod. "Good day, Miss."

"Good afternoon. Is Father in?"

"In the study, Miss."

She thanked him softly and moved through the familiar hush of polished floors and inherited paintings. The study door stood ajar, her father visible within—spectacles low on his nose, the Times rustling like an old friend in his lap.

"Father," she began, lingering at the threshold, "I have some news. I think you'll be quite pleased."

He looked up, amused by her formality. "Oh? What's that, my sweet Mary?"

Letter in hand, she crossed to him before her nerves could second-guess the resolve in her step. "I've been hired. As a doctor. In Northern Alberta."

He adjusted his spectacles, eyes narrowing as he scanned the page. "Canada?"

She nodded. "A one-year posting. There's a need for women doctors in the rural settlements."

He looked up, frowning faintly. "Oh, Mary. We had hoped you might consider something here in Birmingham."

She tried to smile, but it came out thin. "Yes, I thought you might say that."

He folded the letter, slower than necessary. "Canada is hardly civilized. A new country—still wilderness in many parts. You won't have the life you have here. It's... bush and natives."

The phrase struck her like cold water. She turned toward the window, the hedges trimmed to perfection, the garden paths swept and obedient. "I've spoken with Dr. Emma Johnstone. She's practiced there. She says it's difficult—but meaningful."

"Meaningful doesn't pay the bills or keep you safe," he said, rising to pour himself a brandy. "We're speaking of another world, Mary. Settlers, frontier medicine. What if something were to happen to you?"

At that moment, her mother entered, newspapers folded beneath her arm. "What's this about another world?"

Mary turned. "Canada, Mother."

Her mother paused mid-step. "Canada? Surely not."

"It's a year-long government placement in the west. They need doctors—British-trained, Anglican women."

Her mother took a seat, smoothing her skirt with unconscious precision. "Your father is right. It's a world away. It isn't the life we envisioned for you."

She approached them both now, more gently than before. "I understand. But Birmingham has enough doctors. They don't need me. Out there, I can do something vital. I missed my chance with India, and you accepted that."

"We didn't accept it," her mother corrected. "We tolerated it. There's a difference."
Her father took a long sip from his glass. "It's your choice, Mary. But you must understand—it means being far from everyone who loves you."

"I know it does," she said. "But it's only a year. I'll be home by next summer."

Silence followed. Not cold, but dense. Her parents sat like a pair of statues newly conscious of erosion. Finally, her father said, "We'll speak more of this later."

She nodded, letting the stillness settle between them. Her fingers brushed the edge of her coat pocket, where another copy of the letter lay folded. Beyond the walls of that room, the world remained unchanged. But within her, something had already broken open.

Her heart was no longer confined to Birmingham. It was gathering itself, quietly, for departure.

CHAPTER 6

The next day at the hospital unfolded in a blur—charts to update, bandages to change, gentle reassurances whispered over fevers. Mary moved through it all with practiced care, but her thoughts clung to last night's conversation like the damp clings to a wool coat—unshakable, heavy at the seams. The weight of leaving home hadn't lifted, only rearranged itself in her chest.

Still, her hands remained steady. She adjusted a young boy's pillows with a touch that felt more like a promise than a routine act. His smile—missing a front tooth, shy and bright—caught her off guard. Not because it was rare, but because it reminded her why she'd chosen this path. Medicine, at its core, was not efficiency. It was humanity.

Dr. Simmons swept into the ward with his usual clipped stride. "Dr. Percy," he barked, barely glancing at the patients, "you're spending too long with each case. We're behind."

She didn't flinch. "Every patient deserves our full attention, Dr. Simmons. That's how I practice."

He frowned, paused, then walked away without a word. His retreat felt like a line drawn more clearly than any discussion could. As he disappeared down the corridor, her resolve crystallized. She could not practice in a system that rushed healing to meet the clock.

Later, in the warm hush of Dr. Walker's office, sunlight filtered through the blinds in soft golden stripes. Books lined every wall, titles worn from use. He sat behind his desk, sleeves rolled, as if authority and warmth had struck a lifelong truce.

She took a seat opposite him. "Dr. Walker, I've decided. I'm going to Canada."

His expression didn't change—just deepened. "That's brave," he said. "And right."

"I'm nervous," she admitted. "But sure."

He leaned in, resting his forearms on the desk. "You're more than ready. Alberta will test you—but it will also teach you. It will ask everything, and you'll give more than you thought you had."

His words rooted themselves in her. Encouragement, yes—but also a blessing.

"Thank you. For everything," she said.

He rose and came around the desk, placing a firm, fatherly hand on her shoulder. "Canada is lucky to have you. Just remember: this isn't an ending. It's the beginning of your real work."

She left his office lighter—not unburdened, but lifted. For the briefest moment, she imagined herself failing—alone in a snowbound cabin, a life in her hands, and no help coming. The vision flared and vanished. And still, she walked forward.

That afternoon, in the Doctors' Lounge, Henrietta and Clara were already there, chatting over tea and biscuits, journals strewn like breadcrumbs from a day too full. The room, with its worn chairs and familiar scent of antiseptic and strong Earl Grey, offered sanctuary.

Mary joined them, folding herself into a low armchair. "I've made my decision," she said, voice steady.

Henrietta sat up straighter. "You're going."

"I am."

Clara's lips curved into a small, proud smile. "We

thought you might."

"It's official. I leave in a few months."

Henrietta grinned. "And just like that, we'll have to find someone else to steal biscuits for."

Their laughter came easy. But when it quieted, something unspoken lingered.

"I'll miss this," Mary said softly. "I'll miss you both."

Henrietta reached out, squeezing her hand. "We'll write. And you'll write back—with stories. Just don't forget us when you're out there taming wolves and delivering babies by moonlight."

Clara added, "And remember, we're each finding our own path. Yours just starts a little farther away."

As the conversation ebbed, Mary felt a stillness settle inside her. A sense of clarity.

Later, she climbed the stairs to the hospital's rooftop garden. The city sprawled before her, dusk pooling in the spaces between buildings. She sat on a bench, a worn photograph of her family pressed between her fingers.

The edges curled. The ink faded. But the faces—they held.

She traced each one gently, then slipped the photo back into her pocket. A breeze moved through the garden, catching the hem of her coat, carrying with it the scent of lavender and stone.
It was not farewell. Not quite.

When she left the hospital that evening, her silhouette slipped into the amber light. She carried no fanfare, no certainty, only purpose.

And that was enough.

Dr. Mary Percy was ready.

CHAPTER 7

In the span of a few months, her life had become a study in preparation—a season of farewells wrapped in the hushed rustle of folded garments and ticket stubs. Each day passed with the quiet weight of urgency, not frantic but deliberate, as Mary tended to every detail with the same care she once reserved for her patients. The rhythm of her life had shifted, no longer bound by hospital corridors and familiar streets, but by the slow, steady turning toward what lay ahead.

Packing became a ritual. Each item she placed in her trunk held the gravity of memory—a scarf Cecile once borrowed on a windy walk, a worn volume of poetry tucked beside her stethoscope. Letters were signed and sealed, papers sorted into neat stacks. The outward chaos was choreographed; her inner world, less so.

The goodbyes began to collect like postcards—brief

snapshots of affection, joy, and sorrow. Colleagues lingered longer at tea. Patients slipped folded notes into her hands, written in shaky but earnest script. She smiled through them all, but there were moments, especially in the quiet hours, when the permanence of leaving settled over her like dust.

Cecile, steady and luminous, became her anchor. Their days were filled with laughter—tight-lipped at first, then spilling over as they tried to pretend none of it was final. Together they folded dresses and measured out practicality in layers of wool and cotton.

"Three pairs of gloves?" Cecile teased, holding them up like a juggler's props. "Are you moving to the Arctic or auditioning for a silent film?"

Mary smiled, the warmth in her eyes threading through her answer. "Canada's full of surprises. And besides, I've a talent for losing things when I'm nervous."

But the banter couldn't hold back the undertow. Cecile's laughter dimmed. "You know... you're going to be missed. Who'll I trade hospital gossip with when you're out among the wolves?"

They both laughed, but the question lingered, a half-closed door in the conversation. Later, when they found an old photograph—sunlight and wind in their hair, two girls grinning into the future—Mary paused. "Remember that summer? We were so sure the world would wait for us."

"The world doesn't wait," Cecile said. "But real friends don't need it to."

They stood in that silence, the kind only friendship can weather, their eyes saying the rest. As the last clasp clicked shut on her suitcase, Cecile pressed a leather-bound journal into her hand.

"Take this. Write everything down. So when you come back, you won't forget any of it."

Mary nodded, clutching it as if it were already full. "You've packed up half my life today. It's only fair you send me off with a place to unpack it."

The morning of departure came not with fanfare, but with the soft murmur of resolve. Her footsteps on the stairs were steady, her breath anchored by intention. At the foot of the staircase, her father waited. He held an envelope, his fingers smoothing its edge like a man memorizing the act.

"It's for your return," he said. "In case... you need a way back."

She hesitated, met his eyes. "I'll make it there. I don't plan on needing this. But I thank you—for believing I might."

He offered it again, gently. She took it this time, a quiet truce between hope and protection.

Her mother pulled her into an embrace, her perfume soft and familiar. "Write to us, my darling. Tell us everything. You're taking more than our hopes—you're taking our hearts."

Mary swallowed the lump in her throat. "I promise. Every letter will carry a piece of me back to you."

Her father added, "You've always been the brave one. But remember—home is never closed to you."

She hugged them both tightly, breathing in the shape of this moment—the last of its kind.

The cab waited. She stepped outside, the world sharpened by the stillness of parting. Her trunk was loaded, her coat fastened, her gloved hand raised in farewell.

The taxi pulled away. Her parents stood like punctuation marks at the end of a long sentence.

As the city blurred past, she held the journal in her lap and the envelope in her coat. One, a promise. The other, a tether.

Her thoughts turned toward snow-laced pines and distant skylines. Toward the unknown.

Toward a life already calling her forward.

CHAPTER 8

The atmosphere at Southampton's wharf trembled with the energy of departure. Steam hissed from the belly of the great ship, gulls shrieked above the clamor of trunks and voices, and all around Mary stretched the pageantry of parting —tight embraces, tear-stained farewells, laughter pitched too high to be casual. Humanity in its most naked, beautiful disorder.

As the cab weaved through the crowd, her breath caught at the sight of the S.S. Empress of Scotland. She was a leviathan of rivets and iron, poised to cleave the Atlantic in pursuit of other worlds. Her fingers tensed in her lap. So much had been imagined, but now—now it was real.

The steward met her with calm efficiency. Her trunk disappeared in the choreography of the quay, swallowed by practiced hands. This moment—this passage from girlhood to something stranger and braver—was written not in ceremony, but in footsteps and signatures.

She followed the steward aboard. Wood gave way to carpet, the din of the wharf muted by the hush of corridors. The air shifted—less soot, more lavender oil and varnish. Fellow passengers nodded in passing, the language of civility woven into every gesture. Her boots made no sound on the plush runner, but her heart beat loudly enough to mark the occasion.

In her cabin, the steward gestured to the fittings. "Closets here. Drawers there. And the head, miss—powder room, that is."

She nodded, grateful for the clarification. "Thank you."

With a click, the key was placed on the bureau and he was gone. She stood alone, the hum of the ship vibrating beneath her soles, a low, constant promise. The walls gleamed with mahogany trim. The bed, narrow but neat, invited her like a punctuation mark at the end of a long paragraph.

She sat, exhaling for the first time in what felt like hours. The air smelled of salt and polish and beginnings.

Laughter rang in the hallway—bright, feminine, uncontainable. A moment later, the cabin door flew open.

"Percy!" came the delighted cry. "You're here!"

Dr. Elizabeth Rodger burst in with the effervescence of champagne, followed closely by the taller, drier-witted Helen O'Brien.

"We were beginning to think we'd been stood up," Helen said, a mock scowl poorly hiding her grin.

Mary rose, laughing. "Well, I do enjoy making an entrance. Though truth be told, I'm more stunned than stylish at the moment."

Elizabeth flung her arms wide. "Welcome to the finest cabin this side of steerage—and the only one with a medical license in every bed."

Helen gestured to the top bunk with the gallows humor of one who'd already accepted her fate. "Guess who lost the coin toss?"

"You're a good sport," Mary offered.

"I'm a martyr," Helen replied. "And I snore. So consider yourselves warned."

They laughed, the kind of laughter that builds trust in increments. In that small space, something began to weave between them—sisterhood, perhaps, or simply the relief of not having to be brave alone.

The conversation soon turned to the evening meal.

"We must dazzle," Elizabeth declared, already rifling through her trunk. "Let the gentlemen choke on their consommé."

Helen raised an eyebrow. "I've packed one decent dress and a questionable hairbrush. Dazzling will be theoretical."

Mary smiled as she pulled out a modest velvet frock. "I brought pearls. They're not real, but the sentiment is."

Their preparations unfolded like theatre—the rustle of silks, the clink of hairpins, perfume loosed into the air like a spell. The ship's engines pulsed beneath their feet, slow and steady, like a heart bracing for movement.

In the mirror, three faces bloomed into anticipation. Mary's eyes caught her reflection longer than the others—poised, composed, but somewhere beneath, she glimpsed the shadow of everything she was leaving behind. And still, she stood straighter.

"Shall we?" Elizabeth said.

They stepped into the corridor, arms linked. The ship rocked gently beneath them, not yet at sea but already adrift from their old lives.

Behind them, the cabin door clicked shut. Ahead, the ocean waited—not just water, but a vast and unfamiliar future, blue and uncertain and wide enough for reinvention.

CHAPTER 9

In the grand dining room, chandeliers cast nets of light across polished cutlery and crystal goblets, refracting radiance onto linen as crisp as new snow. It was less a room than a performance, and their entrance—arm in arm, dresses whispering like silk secrets—was met with a few lingering glances and the subtle hush that follows elegance.

The maître d', a man of immaculate bearing and polished vowels, greeted them with deference edged in curiosity. When their titles were spoken aloud —Dr. Percy, Dr. O'Brien, Dr. Rodger—his posture straightened further. He led them to their table, not with the briskness of duty, but with the ceremony of reverence.

"Your table, Doctors," he said, bowing slightly. The acknowledgment shimmered between them, not ostentatious, but grounding. Mary felt it like an invisible decoration. A flicker of pride rose—earned, not gifted—but beneath it, a quiet question stirred: who would she become, once this voyage ended and the work began?

The orchestra struck a quiet chord, and the room unfurled its many conversations like silk fans. Around them, the ship's elite murmured over menus and flirted behind champagne flutes. But here, at this table of three, the air buzzed with something different—ambition braided with anticipation, a current beneath the candlelight.

Elizabeth leaned in, eyes bright. "Can you believe this? A palace at sea. All this grandeur—and us, bound for the wilds."

Helen gave a wry smile. "I'll enjoy it while it lasts. Once we hit Alberta, it's porridge and pragmatism."

Mary smoothed her napkin. "Then let's memorize every moment. Tonight, we're queens in exile."

Menus opened like hymnals. Elizabeth, hungry for both adventure and oysters, ordered boldly. "Lobster bisque, filet mignon, and your best Bordeaux."

Helen kept to earthier fare. "Vegetable soup and chicken, please. And perhaps a glass of something that won't knock me overboard."

Mary, eyes scanning the gilded descriptions, landed on a promise of indulgence. "Oysters Rockefeller. Then the salmon. And a glass of white."

The waiter departed with the grace of a man who knew stories began over supper.

Elizabeth raised her glass. "To first chapters, to daring women, to journeys worth the telling."

Their glasses met with a chime that lingered, a note that rang of things just beginning. Mary sipped, and the taste was strange and bright—elegant, yes, but unfamiliar. It struck her how quickly new things could become precious. And how quickly precious things could disappear.

Each dish arrived as a small miracle—creamy bisques that whispered of coastal markets, meats carved like sculpture, sauces that lingered on the tongue. Wines opened in velvet waves. Conversation darted from university tales to imagined futures. She found herself laughing more than she expected. Found, too, that courage need not be quiet. It could sparkle in candlelight and slip between courses like a secret shared.

Still, as Helen recounted a story about a runaway patient, Mary's thoughts began to drift. She imagined her mother at breakfast, the scent of lavender soap mingling with toast and tea. The weight of her father's envelope, tucked in her coat pocket, pressed faintly against her ribs. Birmingham slipped further from her, not just in miles but in substance—like the vanishing edge of a continent. Was she moving toward something larger, or simply away from a life that had grown too narrow to hold her?

Later, on the deck, the wind swept through their hair,

tugging gently at hems and thoughts. The stars had gathered in a fierce chorus above them, bold against the ink of night. The sea breathed around the ship, a restless companion.

"Have you ever seen so many?" Mary asked, her voice hushed.

Helen tipped her face upward. "Not outside of dreams. They don't do this over rooftops in Birmingham."

Elizabeth pointed to the heavens. "Just wait. The Northern Lights. The sky waltzing in green and violet. Canada has its own magic."

Mary's eyes sparkled. "Then I hope it invites us to dance."

And so they did, spinning slowly beneath the stars, their laughter carried off by the wind. The promenade, lit by moonlight and the flicker of distant cigars, transformed. They weren't passengers now, or even doctors. They were women poised on the edge of becoming, dancing on the deck of a world about to open.

Mary, twirling, caught her own reflection in the darkened window—pearls catching the light, cheeks flushed, a smile she didn't recognize. Not because it was false, but because it was new. A different version of herself, surfacing.

She was leaving. Truly leaving. And at last, something in her loosened.

Enough to let the salt air in.

CHAPTER 10

The first full day at sea was less a beginning than a baptism. What had sparkled with orchestral charm the night before now bucked beneath grey skies, the S.S. Empress groaning against the Atlantic's heaving pulse. Wind clawed at the promenade deck, salt and fury entwined. The sea, vast and previously romantic, now rose in jagged rhythm, each wave a rebuke.

In the cabin, Mary clutched a life preserver as though it were a verdict. The room, usually composed in mahogany trim and brass polish, had devolved into chaos. Bottles rolled like dice. The mirror swung on its hinge with every lurch of the ship. Elizabeth, pale and stricken, had surrendered to the powder room with a dignity only slightly intact.

Mary tried to will herself still, as though stillness could anchor the body against the roiling world. But the bed shifted beneath her like something untamed.

The walls thudded and groaned. Outside, the storm scraped its nails along the hull.

She crawled toward the porthole, hoping for some visual reprieve. But the glass wore a mask of seawater, the world beyond it drowned in motion. She saw nothing but the blur of a world unmoored.

In the cramped quarters, the storm became an intimacy. Retching, groaning, the unspeakable solidarity of shared discomfort. Elizabeth's voice floated weakly through the thin wood. "Is it always like this?"

Mary didn't answer. She didn't know. But for a moment—an awful, flickering moment—she wished the ship would sink. Not out of despair, but to end the war between motion and meaning. Then the thought passed, absurd and revealing.

By Tuesday evening, the ship staggered free of the worst. Dawn on Wednesday was calm, almost shamefully so. The sea, smoothed by morning light, mirrored a false serenity. But the damage lingered in bodies and sleep, in linens twisted from restless nights.

Elizabeth emerged from her private hell, disheveled but undefeated. "I dreamt I was being turned inside out."

"You were," Mary said, with a smile that only half-masked her own unraveling.
"Devil's Hole, they call it," Elizabeth muttered. "A name like that should come with a warning painted on the hull."

Mary nodded. "A sailor told me it's where seven currents collide. It makes monsters of the sea."

They laughed, dry-mouthed, but the worst had passed. Mary had eaten during the storm—not out of hunger, but defiance. Two meals down, thirty-six hours of nausea and dread behind her. But survival wasn't the same as endurance. One simply kept breathing; the other meant stepping ashore as someone slightly rearranged. And if she had changed, she couldn't yet name how.

Later, on the promenade, the world tilted back toward civility. The deck, once host to elemental warfare, now welcomed feet in polished shoes. The sun played gently on the brass rails. A gull followed in the ship's wake like a benediction.

Elizabeth joined her, the ghost of storm still clinging to her shoulders, though already retreating. They walked in silence until the cold air, rather than punishing, began to cleanse.

"It's all real now, isn't it?" Elizabeth said. "Not just the ticket or the trunk or the talk. We're doing it. We're gone."

Mary looked out at the blue that stretched like a sentence not yet ended. "Yes," she said. "We are."
They passed through the brass-framed doors, the ship's warm interior embracing them like memory. Uniformed crew nodded with practiced ease, as if calm had always ruled these halls. The breakfast salon shimmered with morning light, the air steeped in coffee and the faint sweetness of baked bread. Linen-covered tables waited like open arms, promising comfort in the aftermath.

She eased into her chair, feeling not the weight of the sea, but the ghost of it. The sea still murmured in her knees, a phantom tide not yet spent. The waiter appeared with practiced poise. Behind him, sunlight spread in softened squares across the carpet.

"To calm waters," Elizabeth said, lifting her cup.

"And steadier stomachs," Mary replied, touching hers to it.

She began to recount all Elizabeth had missed: the storm-tossed meals, the pianist who played despite the lurching keys, the group of passengers who attempted to dance mid-swell, as though defiance could anchor them.

Elizabeth listened with the wide-eyed wonder of

someone returned from the underworld. When Mary described the evening dinners—seven courses, candlelit decadence defying the deep—Elizabeth let out a theatrical sigh. "You mean I missed lamb in port reduction for dry heaves and tile grout?"

They laughed. It was a kind of baptism too.
Talk shifted. Helen, blessed by chance with her own cabin, had slept through the worst. "She didn't even lose a hairpin," Mary said. "Lucky woman."

Their conversation meandered through breakfast—coffee refills, sweet preserves, warm bread. There was talk of delays in Quebec, of detours through Calgary. Of train tickets and missed connections.

"Well," Elizabeth said, buttering toast with theatrical optimism, "what's an adventure without a misstep or two?"

Mary nodded. But her eyes wandered to the window. Cape Race was ahead. And beyond that, land. A line on the horizon that would not tilt.

"I hope we see icebergs," she said. "I want to see something older than all of us."

Elizabeth raised her cup again. "Then to frozen monuments and fresh starts."

The clink of porcelain. The sea, for now, kind. And

Mary, steadier than she had been, though not yet still.

CHAPTER 11

Helen emerged like a survivor of some quiet war, thinner, paler, but upright and moving. After days confined to her cabin, gripped by a seasickness that seemed to rewrite time, she stepped into the breakfast salon as though crossing a threshold back into the living.

Mary spotted her first. Her smile bloomed instantly, warm and wide. "Look who decided to rejoin the land of the upright."

Helen's return smile was wan but game. "Someone had to keep the powder room company. I fear it's grown quite attached to me."

Elizabeth leaned back in her chair, her relief hidden in mock sternness. "You've missed everything, Helen. We've been drinking too much coffee and chasing icebergs without you."

Helen eased into the seat they'd kept open for her,

still negotiating the rhythm of the ship beneath her feet. "While you were spotting icebergs, I was having intimate conversations with the ceiling. And the floor. And anything that didn't move."

Mary poured her a cup of coffee with the reverence of a returning ritual. "Welcome back. Strong and hot, the way the doctor ordered."

Helen accepted it like communion. "If this doesn't cure me, nothing will. Just—spare me the sea tales—my stomach's still negotiating terms."

Elizabeth's voice softened. "We really were worried. You missed some of the worst of it—and some of the best."

Helen nodded, wrapping both hands around the warm mug. "I lived my own private storm. But I'm done with that. I intend to stay upright and enjoy what's left of this adventure. Preferably without revisiting breakfast."

Mary grinned. "You've returned just in time. Elizabeth thinks she saw a berg last night. I think it was moonlight on a cloud."

Helen raised a brow. "An iceberg? Now that, I could get on board with." A pause, then a sly smile. "Pun entirely intended."

Their laughter was easy now, the kind that comes when sickness recedes and friendship fills the room like sunlight. The ship moved steadily through calm waters, but the real steadiness, Mary thought, came from this: three women, side by side again, charting something like a future.

CHAPTER 12

The next day arrived veiled in stillness. The Atlantic, having exhausted its rage, now lay hushed beneath a gauze of fog. The S.S. Empress hovered in place, its engines silenced, suspended in an ocean of milk-white air. Icebergs and fog had conspired to delay them, pushing Quebec landfall to Sunday. Yet Mary, despite the idle hours, felt buoyed by the thrill of proximity to things ancient and cold.

Bundled in sensible wool and a touch of defiance, she stepped onto the deck with Helen and Elizabeth. The air bit at their faces, briny and sharp, and the foghorn moaned through the mist like a warning from another world. Mary wrapped a ship's blanket around her shoulders, its coarse wool a modest defense against the damp.

"One of my great hopes," she said, her voice hushed but sincere, "is to see an iceberg. The steward says it's the season for them."

Helen blinked. "No, really?"

Mary nodded, eyes scanning the pale horizon. Elizabeth leaned closer. "He said they once had to stop and reverse to avoid one. The whole ship stalled mid-Atlantic."

Helen's face pinched with dread. "Oh my goodness. You don't think we'll hit one?"

Elizabeth rolled her eyes. "Helen!"

Mary, more gently: "We've been stationary since sometime in the night. It's just past breakfast now. I imagine we're waiting for a path to clear."

Helen hugged her arms. "It's eerie, this quiet."

Just then the foghorn bellowed, splitting the silence. All three of them jumped, then dissolved into laughter, startled out of their nerves.

"Everyone keeps mentioning the Titanic," Elizabeth said, voice low.

Mary's tone softened. "We've stopped. That's what matters. We're not drifting blind. They're watching."

High above, a sailor stood in the crow's nest, still as a question mark. Below, crew moved with practiced vigilance, their silhouettes cutting through the fog like phantoms.

By afternoon, the mist began to lift. Mary returned to the Promenade Deck, drawn by instinct. And there it was—a massive iceberg, hovering a quarter mile off, ghostly white streaked with a sea-glass green. It shimmered like a cathedral born of cold and time. She stood in reverent silence, breath caught between awe and humility.

Other passengers gathered, their murmurs reverent, almost religious. Then came the low thunder of the engines, slow and sure, and the ship began to move again. The cheer that rose was collective, joyful, a celebration of forward motion.

The fog dissolved like memory. Sunlight pierced the clouds, gilding the deck in warmth. She stood at the rail as the Empress glided toward the Saint Lawrence River, its waters wide and regal. Mountains emerged from the haze, solemn and immense. The terrain surprised her—not the wilderness she expected, but green and dignified, more like Cumberland than the edge of empire. It stirred something homesick and strange inside her.

For two days, the river wound beside them, broad as a vow. On one bank, only forest. On the other, the architecture of a new world, foreign but promising.

Despite the delays, the voyage felt charmed. Customs officers handled their luggage with care; the compartments were tagged and protected. Government arrangements eased their path, smoothing transitions and unlocking doors. A stop in Ottawa had been planned. An interview awaited with Dr. Helen McMurchy, Chief of Maternity and Child Welfare. After that, the Trans-Canada Express.

She felt it all building toward something. The fatigue that nestled behind her eyes could not erase the undercurrent of momentum.

As the ship prepared for its final leg on Tuesday, she lingered at the rail a moment longer, watching the sun lift against the folds of eastern sky.

She was not the same woman who had boarded the Empress in Liverpool. The journey had reshaped her —with its tempests, its silences, its revelations of ice and fog and friendship. And ahead, still, a continent waiting to be crossed.

CHAPTER 13

In the glow of the morning, Quebec City revealed itself to them as their vessel neared the harbor. The view was picturesque, with the grandeur of Château Frontenac towering above, setting a majestic backdrop. Tugboats approached, skillfully assisting the ship to its berth, while onlookers on the deck eagerly watched the city come into view, its architectural beauty unfolding before them.

Once the ship's engines ceased, signaling their arrival, the group made their way down to the wharf, stepping onto land after their lengthy journey across the sea. The cool air greeted them—brisk, clean, full of the day's potential. The planks of the wharf felt firmer than any floor Mary had known in days. She half expected the ground to sway beneath her—but it didn't. She was here. Canada. And the stillness beneath her boots carried the strange, thrilling finality of arrival.

The wharf was bustling, alive with the energy of newcomers and locals alike, the sound of greetings, farewells, and the hustle of transportation filling the air. The ship's luggage steward, along with a team of young helpers, efficiently organized the luggage, ensuring everything was accounted for and loaded onto a truck destined for the train station.

Clad in attire suitable for a day's adventure, the women clustered around the luggage steward who, with a hint of a French accent characteristic of the city, handed them their claim tickets. "Here are your claim tickets for your luggage. It is all being transported to the train. You have about two hours here in the city before you must head to the train for your departure." His instructions were a melodious reminder of their setting in a French-speaking locale.

Mary tipped the porter, then turned to her companions, eyes bright. "Ladies? Are we ready for our first experience with Canada?"

Elizabeth, catching the infectious spirit of adventure, playfully responded, "Oui, oui, mademoiselle," setting their laughter loose like birds startled from a square. Their path might have been uncertain, yet the thrill of exploration propelled them forward.

Stepping onto the bustling streets, they signaled for a taxi, which promptly arrived. With an exchange of eager smiles and a flurry of gestures, they climbed in. The taxi wove through Quebec City's historic lanes, with the majestic Château Frontenac standing grandly in the distance, a beacon guiding their exploration.

For all its elegance, the city felt foreign—but not unwelcoming. Mary wondered whether belonging could grow like ivy: slowly, but with intent.

The few fleeting hours in Quebec City etched themselves onto the canvas of her memory. Scrambling back to the train in the nick of time, they hastened to their seats as the locomotive gave its inaugural jolt, playfully jostling their belongings.

Surrounded by the comfort of first class, the purser navigated through the carriage, attending to the drink requests of Mary and her companions. The gentle sound of glasses clinking together served as a harmonious accompaniment to the train's steady motion. Settling into her seat, her attention was drawn to the Canadian landscape rolling by outside her window, each scene a fleeting piece of a larger, mesmerizing tableau.

Yet her immersion in the passing scenery was briefly interrupted by the smudged window, dulled by a layer of coal dust. With a slight frown, she remarked, "This train may boast a first-class label, but it's shockingly dirty." Despite the minor inconvenience, her enthusiasm remained undiminished. She leaned back, ready to recount the details of their morning adventures.

"Reverend Thompson was like a guardian angel. He

navigated our luggage through customs effortlessly, and Miss Tremaine from the Red Cross gave us a reception fit for queens. Can you believe it?" she said, delight coloring her voice.

Elizabeth, sipping her tea, smiled. "Quite the introduction to Quebec, indeed."

Mary, attempting to add a playful touch, mimicked a French accent. "Quebec is enchanting, truly, but oh so French. Everything from the architecture to the ads breathed French culture—especially around Château Frontenac. And the river views were simply mesmerizing."

Their exchange of smiles continued.

Elizabeth teased, "Mary, your French accent might not be as captivating as Quebec itself."

Helen, barely holding back her laughter, joined in, "Do share, Mary. How did the locals react to your French?"

She laughed with them, conceding, "Well, my French might have been more amusing than accurate. But the locals seemed to enjoy—or at least, humor—my efforts."

Helen added, "I witnessed it firsthand, and let's just say, the locals were exceedingly kind."

"I gave it a try," Mary admitted. "Though my French certainly could use some improvement."

Elizabeth, ever the jester, offered, "When in doubt, just

throw in a French accent and act as if you're fluent. Who needs the actual language, right?"

Their laughter filled the cabin.

Mary then reminisced, "We almost wandered into the Château demanding ice cream at eight in the morning. Can you imagine their faces?"

Elizabeth laughed, "Ice cream at that hour would have indeed been daring."

Helen, who had listened more than she spoke, chimed in, "I'm just relieved we didn't go through with it. The day gave us enough to remember already."

As the train continued its journey, their cabin was alive with shared stories and laughter. Mary, ever curious, wondered about their next stop. "Montreal awaits us. Any ideas on what we should explore?"

Elizabeth was ready for anything. "Perhaps Old Montreal or Mount Royal Park? I'm up for any adventure."

In that fleeting moment between Quebec City and Montreal, the three friends were united by the thrill of exploration and the comfort of each other's company. As the train rolled forward, it wasn't the wheels but their laughter that stitched the miles together.

CHAPTER 14

Three hours later, the train exhaled into Montreal's station, releasing a plume of steam that curled around their ankles like stage fog. They stepped into the heart of Montreal, a city alive with contradictions—a metropolis where French elegance rubbed shoulders with North American bustle. It kept time with the Jazz Age—its modern ambition hemmed in old-world lace.

Mary felt it before she saw it. The city's rhythm—quicker, more syncopated—reverberated through the cobblestones beneath her feet. It was bracing. Disorienting. Exhilarating. For all its charm, Montreal felt charged with something unspoken, a tension between past and progress, tradition and transformation. She could feel it in the clipped gait of passersby, in the jostle of English and French like dancers who refused to lead, and in the narrow glances exchanged across language lines.
"Oh, look at this! It's like we've stepped right into

Paris," she said, eyes wide as she took in the facades and the fashionable silhouettes passing by.

Helen looked around with a dreamy expression. "Imagine, ladies—our very own slice of Europe here in Canada. What shall we explore first?"

Elizabeth unfolded a city map with a grin. "I propose Mount Royal Park for the views, then into the heart of the city for lunch."

"A splendid plan!" Mary clapped her hands. "We might even see the river from up there."

As they navigated through the clamor, streetcars clanged and jazz curled out of open windows, the music of a city on the cusp of something new. Flappers with bobbed hair and scandalous lipstick passed by, their laughter glittering like spilled champagne.

Mary studied them, not with envy but curiosity. There was freedom in their sway, an assertion she hadn't quite found in herself. Not yet.

The city wore its past like a second skin—visible, weathered, but not forgotten. Victorian buildings stood beside sleek Art Deco towers, ironwork balconies casting shadows like lace. Helen, ever observant, paused to trace the carvings on a column. "It's a dance, isn't it? This city—old bowing to new, neither quite yielding."

A gust of wind carried the scent of fresh bread. Elizabeth inhaled, eyes closed. "This city appeals to all the senses."

At a corner, a young man juggled onlookers' delight into the air with three bright balls, his performance ephemeral and joyous. Their laughter blended with the street's symphony.

As they ascended Mount Royal Park, the city below shimmered in the afternoon haze. From the overlook, the St. Lawrence wound through the city like a silver thread pulled taut.

"Look how the river stitches it all together," Mary murmured, her voice a mix of wonder and longing.

"It's mesmerizing," Helen replied. "Like it's holding the city in place."

Elizabeth glanced at her guidebook. "We've time. Let's visit St. Joseph's Oratory before the train."

The basilica rose into view, solemn and immense, its dome cradling the pale sky like a benediction. Inside, the light filtered through stained glass in fractured hues. The hush was immediate, thick with reverence.

Mary lingered in a pew. Here, she didn't feel foreign. She felt small in a way that steadied her. Perhaps belonging wasn't about blending in—it was about learning to stand still in unfamiliar places. The memory of fractured light on the scarf outside echoed the windows here, grace in both sacred and secular forms.

"It's so serene," Helen whispered.

Elizabeth, studying a mosaic, added, "A place of faith amidst all that noise."

Later, walking through Old Montreal's cobbled streets, they passed cafés and market stalls, their aromas weaving a sensory tapestry: espresso, pastry, the tang of ripe fruit.

"It's like we've been transported to a little corner of Paris," Mary said.

They paused at a silk stall. Helen haggled with flair, earning both a scarf and the vendor's admiration. Elizabeth grinned. "Who knew you had such talent for this?"

In a tucked-away café, they savored pressed sandwiches and delicate cups of coffee. The city pressed in at the windows, a kaleidoscope of motion.

"Montreal is a revelation," Mary said. "It hums with possibility—but it's not mine. Not yet."

Elizabeth stirred her drink. "Each city sings its own song. Montreal just happens to be in two keys."

Helen, scarf draped elegantly, smiled. "I expect Edmonton will have its own tune. Perhaps one we haven't learned the words to yet."

As golden light softened the day, they returned to the station, Montreal slipping behind them like a dream half-remembered. The city had offered no easy answers—only beauty, tension, and the promise that belonging, like ivy, might one day root—and take hold.

Alberta awaited. And with it, a new kind of music.

CHAPTER 15

Under the expansive daylight, the Montreal train station stood like a cathedral of departure—its robust stone echoing with the ghosts of countless journeys. Here it was, at last: the final leg. Edmonton. Through the Canadian Shield, past the Great Lakes, into the beating heart of the prairies.

Outside, a symphony of motion unfolded—porters racing, voices rising in farewell, the whistle of outbound trains like flung ribbons. Their taxi sighed to a stop. Laden with parcels and memories, the three women emerged, their farewells to the French-speaking driver caught in the hum of anticipation.

Mary glanced up at the station's stone façade. There was no room for hesitation now. "Hurry, ladies. We are late," she called, her voice quick and clear above the din. They threaded through the crowd, propelled by urgency and instinct, moving like women who had already crossed oceans and wouldn't stop now.

Inside the first-class carriage, grandeur softened into comfort: velvet seats, polished fixtures, and a hush of curated calm. A porter approached, smiling with precision. "Are you ladies searching for your seats?"

They handed him their tickets. "This way, ladies, if you please." He led them through the corridor to their private cabin. Gratitude flickered in their eyes as they sank into their seats and released the tension they hadn't known they carried.

The train shuddered to life. Night pressed gently against the windows, casting shadows over the tea service that gleamed on the table. Elizabeth, knitting in a pool of lamplight. Helen, folded into sleep. Mary, coffee in hand, stared past her magazine, her thoughts already further west.

"What do you think it will be like, working in northern Alberta?" Elizabeth asked, her voice low.

Mary blinked back into the room. "I can hardly wait to find out," she whispered. "But I'm not quite sure what we are in for."

"I keep picturing forest and rivers and wildlife," Elizabeth said. "My parents once got a postcard from Canada. A stag, a pine ridge. Everything sunlit."

Mary smiled. "I hope it's that beautiful. The Fellowship gave me contact info before we left. A woman named Kate Brighty is meeting us. Superintendent of Public

Health Nursing. She'll help us settle."

Helen snored softly, a punctuation mark in the quiet. They exchanged a chuckle.

The rhythm of the train became the rhythm of their rest. Sleeping arrangements echoed shipboard habits: Helen in the Pullman. Each morning, the porter knocked with coffee and biscuits.

They'd been rolling west for thirty-six hours, through towns no bigger than breath marks in the trees. Past Sudbury, the wilderness closed around them like a cathedral of green.

The train cut through forest and lake, a silver needle stitching the land together. Mary pointed out the window. "Elizabeth, look. Lakes and woods as far as the eye can see. Rivers catching the light like silk."

She leaned close. The forests shimmered; the lakes gleamed like burnished metal. "It's like being inside a painting."

"We passed Lake Superior this morning," Mary said. "Wrapped in mist. I was too sleepy to really see it. I regret that."

"I can imagine it," Elizabeth said. "Like a veil over something sacred."

The land opened to a great lake, its surface a mirrored sky. They watched in silence, the beauty too vast for speech.

"It's moments like this that remind me how much wonder there is in the world," Mary said.

Elizabeth nodded. "This trip—it's more than travel. It's a kind of becoming."

The day porters appeared like carnival hawkers, their wares absurdly priced.

"All the day porters come along selling cigarettes, fizzy drinks, magazines, fruit," Mary said. "All three times what they should cost. A pot of tea? Twenty-five cents. My lunch today? Nearly two dollars. I'm rationing myself to one meal a day."

Elizabeth looked uneasy. "I wish I'd gotten a typhoid vaccine. They said we wouldn't need it west of Winnipeg, but we haven't reached Winnipeg yet, and I keep drinking water and eating ice cream."

Mary's face darkened. "The ice water tastes fine until you see how it gets here. Hauled in barrels. Chopped with dirty tools. Pushed in with filthy boots. CPR calls this 'effortless perfection.'"

She paused. "And the Third-Class passengers... it's cruel. Seasick on the boat, then herded like cattle. No bedding, stifling heat. Children everywhere."

Elizabeth nodded. "I walked through that car. The smell alone nearly undid me."

Mary's gaze turned toward the window. "Still, the cities... I'm impressed. Clean. Well-dressed people, tree-lined streets. Ottawa is like Paris in the shade. Every girl wears something beautiful. Their skin so pale. I didn't expect it."

The train thundered westward through Northern Ontario. Forests gave way to logged clearings, lakes to scattered towns. The steel serpent threaded the wilderness, a flicker of modernity across an ancient land. Children waved. Trees bowed in passing.

At dusk, the prairie declared itself—open sky, gold fields, horizon held like breath. The train slipped forward, an arrow pointed at Edmonton.

Mary rested her forehead against the cool glass. She had crossed half a world and felt it now—not as distance, but as weight. She was no longer arriving. She was becoming.

CHAPTER 16

The train sighed to stillness beneath a sky rinsed in prairie light. As the women stepped onto the platform in Edmonton, the sun greeted them like an old friend—warm, unfiltered, and brimming with possibility. The station pulsed with arrivals and departures, a place where stories brushed shoulders: hellos threaded through goodbyes, futures stitched beside farewells.

In the crowd, two women held a hand-painted sign, its letters softened by travel: Welcome Doctors. Elizabeth spotted it first and touched Mary's arm. "There they are."

They approached with purpose, feet still echoing the rhythm of the rails beneath the soles of their shoes.

"Doctors, welcome to Edmonton," said Katie Brighty, her smile wide, her voice flecked with genuine warmth. "Did you have a pleasant journey?"

Mary extended a hand. "The journey was an adventure in its own right. I'm Mary Percy—it's a pleasure to finally meet you."

Introductions moved swiftly, like a breeze stirring loose pages. Olive Watherston flagged down a porter and directed the transfer of trunks and parcels, her efficiency offset by a kindness that made Mary feel less like a visitor, more like someone returning to a place she'd never been.

As they moved toward the street, Katie leaned in with a touch of conspiratorial charm. "Tomorrow, you'll meet the Honourable George Hoadley, Minister of Health, at the Parliament Buildings."

Olive added, "And Dr. Margaret Owens—one of ours—is already waiting at the Women's Hostel."

Near the waiting Hudson sedan, Helen grinned. "Olive, should we expect a grand reception at the hostel? Perhaps even a warm bath and some soap?" Her voice carried the sparkle of arrival.

Olive smiled back, the corners of her mouth tilting just enough to promise something more. "You may be surprised. We've prepared a few comforts—enough, I hope, to make you feel you've arrived."

Their laughter scattered into the hum of the city, mingling with taxi horns, pigeon wings, and the scrape of luggage wheels on concrete. For Mary, Edmonton didn't feel like a threshold. It felt like breath after holding one.

At dawn, the city unfurled beneath a golden haze. The women stepped out of the hostel, faces turned to the new day. A breeze rustled the poplars. Chimney smoke curled above the roofs like ink in water.

Helen, stretching, said, "So—how did you sleep?"

Elizabeth exhaled deeply. "The bed didn't move. That alone felt like a miracle."

Mary raised an eyebrow. "Yes, well, one of us was snoring like a grain elevator at full tilt. Elizabeth, care to confess?"

"It wasn't me!" she said, mock-offended. "Must've been one of the other girls."

A black car idled at the curb, its windows catching the sun. The driver already knew their names. As they climbed in, Mary paused, hand on the doorframe, gaze on the brightening sky.

She had crossed half a world—and felt it now, not as distance, but as gravity. She was no longer arriving. She was becoming.

"I'm looking forward to meeting the Minister. And Margaret Owens," she said, voice steady.

Helen leaned back, eyes sparkling. "Do you think he'll offer us cigars like he did with Katie?"

Elizabeth wrinkled her nose. "I'll pass. Though it

would make a memorable first impression."

The car pulled away, their laughter trailing behind like steam from the train that brought them here.

The city waited—not with certainties, but with open hands and wide skies.

CHAPTER 17

The Parliament Buildings stood like a fortress of purpose against the prairie sky, all limestone and glass and late-morning sun. As the women approached, the grandeur of the architecture pulled their gaze upward—its columns, its stateliness, its sheer refusal to be ignored. Even the air seemed quieter in its shadow. Mary felt her heart flutter in the hush, a quiet beat of awe—or was it fear? She steadied herself. There was no going back now.

She paused on the threshold. This was no drawing room in Birmingham. This was power, blunt and unabashed. Inside, the Minister's office offered a contrast—warmth against formality. Polished wood, velvet chairs, and a view that reached past the North Saskatchewan River to the rim of sky.

"Miss Brighty, wonderful to have you back," said the Honourable George Hoadley, Minister of Health, his voice textured with easy command. He crossed the room with a practiced gait, hand extended.

Katie introduced them with poise. "Doctor Mary Percy, from Birmingham."

She stepped forward. "The honour is mine, sir," though her voice trembled ever so slightly, as if aware of just how far she had come—in miles, in meaning.

"Doctor Helen O'Brien, from Dublin."

She smiled, effortless. "Very well, thank you, sir."

"Doctor Elizabeth Rodger, Edinburgh."

The Minister chuckled at the roll of her brogue. "That's quite the accent you carry."

She grinned. "I take great pride in it, sir."

"As well you should," he said, gesturing them to sit. "Let's make ourselves comfortable."

Cigars were lit with ceremony. A small gesture, yet it seemed to signal something larger—access, inclusion, the beginning of real work. The room carried the scent of leather, smoke, and ambition—the kind of air men were used to breathing, but which Mary would have to learn to inhabit.

Mary leaned in toward Elizabeth. "Quite the office, isn't it?"

"A step up from steerage," she murmured.

Helen's gaze had found the wall map—wide stretches

labeled "Unknown Territory."

"So much is left blank," she said.

"Exactly," said Hoadley. He walked to the map, his drink in hand. "That blankness? That's your canvas."

He spoke without haste, letting his words settle. "You won't go directly to your districts. First, you'll rotate—a week or two in varied places. You'll see what's needed. What's missing."

Mary listened, keenly. There was something in his tone—not just bureaucratic foresight, but belief. A rare quality in men of his standing.

"We have a traveling clinic," he went on. "Doctors, dentists, nurses. Tents for surgery, for sleeping. A stove, a gramophone, even an ice chest. You bring the hospital to them."

Helen raised an eyebrow. "Music, too?"

"Spirits must be lifted," he said, smiling. "You'll find that matters."

Elizabeth asked, "How long will we rotate?"

"Long enough to learn. Short enough to keep you moving."

He pointed back to the map. "Alberta needs settlers. Settlers need services. That's where you come in. Not just as doctors. As anchors. As reasons to stay."

Mary felt the weight of it then—not crushing, but clarifying. She had not merely crossed the ocean. She had crossed into purpose.

Helen asked about the field kits.

"You'll have everything," Hoadley said. "Tools for teeth, for babies, for broken bones. And support from us, where it counts."

Elizabeth added, "Will language be an issue?"

"It will be," he answered, plainly. "But we adapt. Nurses learn the tongues. We hire interpreters. You build trust with time and respect."

Mary asked, "What sort of people will we serve?"

He considered. "Farmers. Families. Homesteaders. Some speak Polish. Some Ukrainian. Some Cree or Blackfoot. Some speak the land, if you listen closely."

Helen laughed. "And what of my Irish?"

He raised his glass. "They'll forgive you, if you cure their toothaches."

The conversation loosened, turned personal. They asked how the traveling clinic chose its stops.

"Word spreads," he said. "Our nurses go ahead. They book appointments, spread the news. The clinic follows, like a tide."

Surgery in a tent. Deliveries in snowstorms. Mary

imagined it all—the exhaustion, the cold, the moments of joy so sharp they hurt. She wondered how many would break under that cold. Or be broken by something colder still—silence, grief, the weight of being too far from home.

"Quite frankly," he said, refilling his drink, "it's every woman for herself. But you won't be alone."

She sat straighter. Her throat tightened, not from fear, but from the sudden sense that this room—this moment—was the threshold. And she was stepping through.

When they stood to leave, the Minister offered his hand again.

"Alberta awaits you," he said. "And it needs what you carry."

Outside, the Parliament shimmered in the noon light. The wind tugged gently at Mary's coat. The unknown still loomed. But it no longer felt nameless.

It felt like a call.

CHAPTER 18

The traveling clinic had taken up position near the Municipal Hall in Clyde—a modest town nestled in prairie light, fifty miles north of Edmonton. It was Sunday, the kind of Sunday that moved slowly, with children in white stockings walking home from church and bees tracing lazy loops through wild roses.

In the open field, the tents were rising. One by one, they took shape: a great canvas heart surrounded by smaller outposts, their ropes drawn taut by a rhythm of practiced hands. Crates opened like treasure chests, revealing the bones of a hospital-in-miniature—tables, chairs, stretchers, pillows, surgical trays wrapped in cloth. Blankets were folded with reverence. Electric cables sprawled across the grass like vines, carrying the hum of potential: lights, heat, a cooling chest for precious medicines.

Mary stood watching it all unfold, her sleeves rolled,

her boots dusty. The air was scented with pine, sweat, and the faint metallic tang of machinery. She could still hear Minister Hoadley's voice echoing in her mind: Two dentists, two doctors, four nurses—a mobile lifeline, stitched together by purpose.

Locals mingled easily with the team, driving in nails, lifting canvas, offering bread and berries and tools. It was, her thought, like raising a cathedral of healing. No sermon, no organ—but the same quiet holiness.

By late afternoon, the sun had dipped low enough to turn everything gold. She tied off a final rope and stepped back to admire the scene. "This is quite the setup. I never imagined camping could be so... civilized."

Elizabeth was arranging firewood nearby. "Civilized? I was halfway expecting a butler to emerge from the underbrush with a tray of gin and tonics."

Helen, laying out blankets in a sleeping tent, laughed. "Well, posh or not, this is home for a week. Let's not let the bears in."

They looked around. Silver birch trees stood like quiet sentries. Wild honeysuckle tangled at the edges. Blue lilies peeked from the brush, their petals trembling in the breeze. Even the tents seemed to belong, like mushrooms springing up after rain.

Mary exhaled. "We're making something good here."

Helen nodded. "Yes... and tomorrow, the real work

begins."

As dusk settled over the field and the last mallet blows echoed into quiet, Mary found herself staring at the largest tent. Tomorrow it would fill with pain, with healing, with decisions. She felt the familiar edge of self-doubt flicker—but steadier, too, was the pulse of readiness. She had crossed an ocean. She had chosen this.

And it did. Morning arrived with the hush of expectation. The first patients came as a slow trickle, then a stream—women in kerchiefs, children with sunburned cheeks, farmhands with calloused hands and wary eyes. The district nurse moved with precision, clipboard in hand, directing patients to the right tent. Katie, ever composed, passed them lists, offered updates, fielded concerns.

Mary found herself face-to-face with her first patient before she'd fully caught her breath.

The day unfolded in pulses—examinations, extractions, diagnoses, bandages. The work was both relentless and intimate. She held the hand of a boy while a nurse numbed his gums. She stitched a gash in a man's arm while the patient told her, half-proud, how it happened splitting fence posts.

By late afternoon, the pace had slowed just enough to allow a breath. The three women gathered near the supply tent, cups of coffee in hand.

Elizabeth sank onto a folding stool. "Well, that was something."

Mary wiped her brow, her smile tired but real. "I never thought pulling teeth could feel so personal."

Helen chuckled. "I never knew children could scream with such conviction. I felt like a matador."

Elizabeth raised her cup in mock salute. "To surviving Day One."

Mary looked around at the tents, now humming with the quiet murmur of recovery. "They may not remember our names. But they'll remember they were cared for."

Helen nodded. "Let's just hope they don't remember us as the tooth-pulling monsters of Clyde."

Their laughter rose like smoke, warm and unpretentious, cutting through the fatigue. For a moment, they were not doctors, not strangers in a foreign place. They were women building something, together.

The sun hung low again, casting long shadows across the grass. The tents glowed from within. And in that golden hush between duty and rest, Mary felt it again —that flicker of certainty.

They were doing what they had come to do.

And they were not alone.

CHAPTER 19

The sun had long since slipped beneath the horizon, leaving behind a copper glow that clung to the edges of the sky like memory. Dinner was done. Tin plates scraped clean. Boots loosened. Around the fire, the women sat slouched and quiet, their bodies heavy with the weight of the day, their spirits lit by something harder to extinguish.

The flames crackled, casting shadows that leapt and bowed across their faces. Mary shifted on the log bench, rolling her shoulders, the smell of smoke and iodine still clinging to her sleeves.

"What a day," she murmured, gazing into the darkening sky. "I never imagined we'd see so many patients in such a short span."

Helen exhaled deeply, her hair escaping its pins in wisps. "The variety of cases! I never thought I'd be removing tonsils beside a crate of potatoes."

Elizabeth grinned, wiping her palms on her skirt. "Well, variety is the spice of life. Today we were served a five-course meal."

They laughed—tired laughter, but real—and let the silence stretch between them, companionable and easy. Insects chirred in the tall grass. A loon called from the lake. Somewhere beyond the tents, a child coughed in her sleep.

"This," Mary said, gesturing to the flickering circle of light they shared, "this is why we came. To be useful. To matter."

Helen's gaze lifted to the sky, where the first stars had begun to pierce the velvet dark. "Every stitch, every consultation... It's not just medicine. It's a kind of anchoring. We're helping people stay."

Elizabeth stirred the coals, sparks leaping like fireflies. "Imagine the stories we'll tell one day. 'That time in Clyde, when we sterilized instruments over a camp stove and did rounds with chickens pecking at our boots.'"

More laughter. It cut through the weariness like a knife through gauze.

Beneath the surface of banter, though, ran something quieter—a current of knowing. Of shared fatigue. Of the weight and worth of what they were attempting out here in the margins.

They didn't need to name it. It hung between them like the hush of pines after snowfall—quiet, certain.

The fire popped, and Mary leaned back, gazing into the branches overhead.

"We're not just passing through," she said softly. "We're being marked by this place as much as we're leaving our own mark."

She thought of her father's hands—weathered, unyielding—and how he'd never imagined her here. How she could barely imagine herself, even now. Back in Birmingham, she'd feared stagnation more than hardship. But here, hardship had a face. And somehow, it steadied her. She felt it in the ache of her limbs, in the steadiness of her breath: she was becoming someone new.

Elizabeth, suddenly solemn, nodded. "Who would have thought we'd be here—under this sky, in this wild pocket of the world—changing lives?"

Mary smiled faintly. "Life's full of surprises."

Helen poked at the logs with a stick, sparks rising. "Well, at least we're not short on drama. If our patients only knew the behind-the-scenes chaos..."

Mary tilted her head, listening. The night had gone still. Not silent, but expectant.

Elizabeth followed her gaze into the trees. "Do you

ever feel," she said slowly, "like the universe holds its breath before something shifts?"

Mary nodded, her voice barely above the fire's hiss. "I've learned to listen to that feeling. And tonight... The air feels different. Like the quiet before the wind changes."

Helen let out a dry laugh. "I hope it's not prophetic. I've had my quota of excitement for one day."

But even as they joked, the stillness wrapped around them like a shroud. The firelight danced in their eyes. Shadows stretched long behind them.

They didn't yet know what the hours ahead would demand of them. But the wind did.

And for now, they leaned in close, shoulder to shoulder, three women beneath a sky flung wide with stars. Bone-tired. Soul-lit. Not undone.

Not yet.

CHAPTER 20

The storm arrived like a freight train in the dark—no warning, no mercy. One moment, the camp lay under a hush of starlight; the next, the heavens split open.

Rain pelted the canvas with a percussive fury, thunder cracking in quick succession, each one a rib-rattling drumbeat. Lightning etched the sky in jagged script, illuminating the tents in bursts of eerie silver.

Mary woke to chaos—a world already half-drowned, clawing at the seams.

The flap of her tent had torn loose in the wind, slapping wildly as rain poured in. She bolted upright, heart pounding, feet hitting cold water pooled across the floor. Her blankets—once warm and orderly—were sodden, bunched in retreat from the invasion.

The dark was absolute. Disoriented, she moved by

instinct, hands grasping at canvas, rope, anything. The wind roared in her ears, drowning out her muttered curses. Raindrops tracked down her face like cold fingers. The flap snapped again, and she lunged, catching it just long enough to wrestle it closed, her palms stinging from the effort.

Around her, the storm raged with a kind of sentience—snarling, laughing, lashing like some ancient beast uncaged. She cinched the flap tight, then shoved her meager belongings onto a nearby crate, salvaging what she could from the rising puddle.

Drenched and shivering, she climbed back onto the cot. The blankets clung to her damp skin. Still, she gathered them close. Not for warmth, but for the stubborn ritual of it.

The storm wouldn't be ignored—it shouted and slammed and rattled its teeth against the tent walls. But inside, for a moment, she lay still. Water seeped beneath her, and thunder spoke low and cruel, like a door slamming in an empty church.

There was fear, yes. And annoyance. But also something else—an awe that stirred in her chest like smoke. Here was nature, unfiltered. A force too big to control, too old to reason with. And yet she was here, small and soaked and stubborn, weathering it.
She turned her face toward the canvas ceiling, listening as the wind clawed past. Sleep would not

come. But neither would defeat.

Not tonight.

CHAPTER 21

In the fresh light of day, the remnants of the storm revealed themselves in water-filled impressions across the field, each puddle a small testament to the night's violence. The clinic—so recently a locus of purpose and urgency—was now entering its final phase. The work had shifted: from healing to dismantling, from holding ground to moving forward. People moved deliberately, boxing supplies, striking the tents, hoisting crates onto waiting trucks. The air was filled with the scent of damp canvas, sizzling bacon, and something quieter still—the bittersweet gravity of departure.

Mary emerged from her tent into this fractured calm, squinting into the sunlight. Her boot found an ankle-deep puddle with a slap of cold surprise. She let out a gasp, danced a half-step backward, and surveyed her mud-streaked fate with a grimace that turned quickly into a reluctant smile.

"Well," she muttered, flicking moisture from her hem, "if that's not a prairie baptism, I don't know what is."

Elizabeth, bright-eyed and already halfway packed, called out from behind a folded tent flap. "Looks like Clyde wanted to give you a proper send-off."

Helen trailed after, lugging her satchel with the resigned grace of someone who had not slept much. "Honestly, your boots were far too clean," she said. "It was making the rest of us look bad."

Mary lifted her sodden foot and examined the squelching mess of leather and muck. "Consider them properly broken in," she replied. "Now if I could only say the same for myself."

"Coffee first," Elizabeth announced. "Then penance."

They crossed the field in tandem, dodging glistening ruts and hidden pools, the earth soft and treacherous beneath their steps. A local man, sleeves rolled and boots caked with clay, intercepted them with a smile and an outstretched arm.

"Doc," he said, addressing Mary, "we've got coffee brewing under the shelter. Strong enough to wake the dead. Come warm up."

Gratitude rose in her like steam. "You're a saint," she said, clasping the tin mug he handed her like it was sacred.

Around them, the field buzzed with practiced

motion, everyone moving like they'd done this before in another life. Locals and nurses, medics and farmhands, all worked together without ceremony, a kind of unspoken choreography born of shared experience. The tent's canvas belly shrank with every tug of rope, each collapse punctuated by bursts of laughter and shouted instructions.

She sipped the coffee and watched it all. The storm had rattled them, yes—but it had not undone them.

A wiry man in a cap paused beside her, wiping his brow. "You know, we haven't had real rain like that in weeks. Fields needed it, sure. But you folks headed to Jarvie?"

She nodded. "That's the plan. Why?"

He gave a dry chuckle. "Well, if you thought last night was rough, wait 'til your tires hit those roads. Mud deep enough to swallow a wagon whole."

Helen, overhearing, groaned softly. "Do tell."

He grinned. "Chains on the wheels, spades in the trunk, maybe a prayer or two. And if you get stuck—and you will—cut yourself a tree, jam it under the tire, and hope she bites."

Elizabeth took a long drink of coffee. "Charming. Sounds like adventure with extra steps."

But Mary only nodded, her gaze drifting past the horizon. The field, the mud, the laughter—they were all prelude. The storm had been only the beginning.

They were leaving something behind here, yes. But they were also carrying it with them: the grit, the joy, the quiet ache of having made a difference. The road ahead would test more than their skill. It would ask for everything they had.

The traveling clinic, forged in urgency and hope, was now a crucible. And in the coming days, it would reveal who they had become—not just as healers, but as women.

And so, with boots sodden and spirits high, they readied for what lay ahead.

CHAPTER 22

At four o'clock, the clinic caravan pulled away from Clyde, its wheels still damp with gratitude and goodbyes. Spirits ran high—but the road north proved quickly indifferent to their optimism. Within minutes, progress slowed to a crawl.

The so-called Peace River Highway, more aspiration than infrastructure, had been rendered a quagmire by the previous night's storm. Vehicles that once moved with certainty now lumbered through the mire, beasts hobbled by nature's grip. Wheels spun and choked; engines groaned in protest.

Sunlight bore down from a cloudless sky, merciless and bright. Mud clung like a second skin, thick and reluctant. Elizabeth took the wheel of the Essex, her jaw set. "This is quite the driving test," she muttered, trying to keep the mood light.
From the back, Mary let out a rueful laugh. "Who

knew mud could make such an impression?"

Helen, wedged among cases of medical supplies, groaned. "And to think, all this for the noble cause of sore throats and splinters."

The Essex lurched again. Elizabeth gripped the wheel tighter. "You two get to relax back there, but this thing's fighting me like a mule."

Mary glanced in the rearview mirror, sympathy edged with envy. She didn't like feeling useless—but there was no room to switch places. "Just keep it moving," she said. "Stopping's the kiss of death."

They made it eighteen miles in three hours.

When the small truck ahead finally surrendered to the mud, the Ford went in to assist—and was promptly swallowed whole.

Farther up, the Studebaker bucked and spun, trapped in its own battle. After half an hour of backbreaking effort, it was finally pulled free, only to sink again trying to rescue another.

As the Essex rolled to a stop behind the chaos, Mary stared ahead. The road shimmered with heat and futility. "We're next, aren't we?"

"Let's hope not," Elizabeth replied.

But when the Studebaker's driver jogged over, his boots slick with sludge, hope thinned.

"We tried to pull the truck, but got stuck ourselves," he said. "Are you stuck too?"

"I haven't moved yet," Elizabeth said. "Was waiting for the show to end."

"Start moving. And don't stop."

The Essex surged forward, miraculously finding grip. "Don't stop, don't stop," the man shouted, jogging beside the car.

Mary and Helen clung to their seats as Elizabeth steered, determination etched across her brow. Mary studied her face—concentration like flint, shoulders hunched with the weight of progress. She envied that kind of clarity. Out here, everything she thought she knew—about control, preparedness, competence—was mired in the same mud.

Then came the sound—a squelch, a yell. The man slipped, face-first into the mud, his pride more bruised than anything else.

Laughter burst from the Essex, cutting through the tension.

They kept moving.

"Farm up ahead," Mary pointed. "Maybe we can get help."

Elizabeth leaned to see—but the Essex rolled to a reluctant stop.

"No! No, no, no," she groaned.

She reversed. Nudged forward. The tires only hissed, then gave up.

"We walk," she said flatly.

Boots hit the mud. Skirts lifted. The road swallowed them ankle-deep. It took thirty minutes to walk half a mile. By the time they reached the farm, they were soaked in sweat and silence.

Mary walked behind the others, her legs aching, mud weighing down each step like doubt. Was this the calling she had longed for? The romance of remote medicine felt laughably distant, lost beneath the weight of her own body slogging forward. But still—she moved.

They returned with horses and farmhands. The scene they'd left had worsened: two cars mired, the truck now invisible behind a mile of uncooperative road.

The men—exhausted, silent—watched as help arrived. There was no celebration, no speeches. Just a quiet exchange of burden.

As dusk fell, seven horses and eight men labored to free the truck. Mud sucked at every step. At ten o'clock, they sent for a tractor.

It arrived at eleven o'clock—chugging, iron-lunged, unflinching. The caravan crawled forward behind it, twelve more miles through blackened prairie and rutted, unforgiving track.

At three o'clock in the morning, the truck stuck again. No one swore. No one panicked. They were too tired for drama. Someone spotted telegraph poles nearby, and the men hauled them over to wedge beneath the tires.

Mary, stiff with mud and fatigue, watched it all. Her body had stopped complaining hours ago, resigned to the trial. The prairie wasn't testing their patience—it was measuring their worth. She stood back as the men labored, the stars wheel-spinning silently overhead, and felt herself suspended in something raw and honest. No masks, no theory, no buffers. Just bone, will, and forward motion.

The final mile to Jarvie was made in silence. The Essex rolled in first, then the others. It was six o'clock in the morning—fourteen hours after they'd set out.

Mary stepped from the car, her skirt stiff with dried mud, her limbs leaden. Somewhere beneath the exhaustion, she felt it—the road had asked more of her than muscle. It had asked who she was becoming. But something inside her steadied. They had made it.

No one cheered. But no one needed to. The sun broke over the trees, and the world, for a moment, felt like triumph.

CHAPTER 23

As dawn tiptoed into Jarvie, the clinic caravan rolled into town beneath a pale sky. The vehicles, lacquered in a proud coat of mud, settled in a field by the river—scarred but intact.

A modest clapboard house stood nearby, the home of the District Nurse—Sarah Conlin, one of Alberta's earliest pioneer nurses. She stepped onto the wide porch as the Essex rolled to a stop, wiping her hands on her apron. Her eyes lit up when she spotted the three women emerging, travel-worn and mud-streaked but upright.

"You're my new members of the Travelling Clinic," she called out, voice bright with welcome. "Welcome, welcome—I've been expecting you."

Mary stepped forward, her skirt heavy with dried mud, and extended her hand. "Nurse Conlin—it's good to meet you. I'm Dr. Mary Percy. This is Dr. Elizabeth Rodger and Dr. Helen O'Brien. Miss Brighty said we'd find you here."

The older woman took her hand with a firm grip. "Sarah," she corrected warmly. "None of that formality here—not after the road you've just endured."

She turned to the others, her gaze full of ease and good humor. "You've certainly earned your place. Come in—no canvas tents this stop. You're staying with me while the clinic's in town."

There was a brief, stunned silence.

"Really?" Helen said, blinking. "You're sure?"

Sarah laughed and motioned them inside. "Of course I'm sure. I've got beds, hot water, and a porch that catches the best light in the morning. Besides, you've had enough of the mud for one week."

Relief swept across their faces like a warm wind. Elizabeth gave a soft laugh. "I think I'm going to cry."

"Wait until you've tasted the coffee," Sarah teased. "Come on, let's get you out of those boots."

The sun had begun to rise in earnest, casting soft gold across the wild roses, raspberries, and tangled prairie grass. Sarah paused halfway to the house and tilted her head. "I never get tired of this light. It makes even the mud look like something sacred."

Mary nodded, her voice hushed. "It's beautiful here."

She hadn't realized how tightly she'd been wound until that moment—until the gentleness of this place, this porch, this stranger's welcome, unspooled her. The prairie held no memory of last night's struggles. And yet, in some quiet way, it seemed to recognize them.

Inside, the warmth of the little house wrapped around them like a quilt. The furniture was worn but welcoming, the air steeped in the scent of coffee and sunlight on old wood. Sarah motioned toward a couch. "Sit, sit. You all look like you've danced with the devil and won."

Helen flopped down with a grateful sigh. Elizabeth joined her, easing into the cushions with a groan. Mary stood a moment longer, taking in the shelves lined with tin mugs, stacks of linens, and a corner that hinted at a makeshift clinic.

She had imagined wilderness medicine as relentless. She hadn't imagined it might also be tender.

"Thank you, Sarah," she said softly. "It means a great deal."

Sarah handed out steaming mugs. "Mud, horses, midnight rescues—that's just a regular Tuesday out here. But you made it. And you're very welcome."

"The mud had a personal vendetta," Helen said, shaking her head. "But I suppose it lost."

Mary took a long sip, the heat of the coffee anchoring her back to herself. Beneath the exhaustion, something stirred—something not quite named. This was the life she had wanted, wasn't it? Not the romance of it, but the truth. The fight. The grace.

"And to think, this is just the beginning."

Sarah leaned against the kitchen counter, her mug in hand. "Well, you've passed the test. You'll fit in here just fine."

Then her tone softened. "There are spare beds in the back room. Get some rest. We'll worry about the clothes later."

Gratitude passed between the women in glances and sighs. They had arrived—not just in Jarvie, but into something steadier, quieter, more human.

Later that morning, Mary stirred in a worn armchair, the lace-curtained window throwing pale light across her lap. She stretched, then rose to find Elizabeth already awake, tea in hand.

"Did you sleep?" Elizabeth asked.

"Just enough to want more," Mary replied.

Elizabeth smiled. "Tea? Or that coffee Sarah makes that could revive the dead?"

"Coffee, please."

As Mary sipped from the mug, she peered out at

the slow-moving morning. The clatter of distant hoofbeats, a field rinsed clean, and somewhere nearby—the sound of a door opening, work beginning.

The ache in her legs reminded her of every inch of last night's journey, but her hands, oddly, felt steady. It hadn't broken her. It had carved something out of her instead—made room.

"Helen and Sarah are already at the clinic," Elizabeth said. "Left about half an hour ago."

Mary nodded, the weight of the night settling into something quieter. Something like resolve.

"Let's finish our coffee," she said, rising. "There's work ahead."

CHAPTER 24

By midmorning, the field beside the river had transformed into a small, sun-drenched miracle. The traveling clinic unfurled its canvas like sails on a windless sea, and the town stirred around it—children darting between chairs, elders in Sunday coats waiting patiently in line, laughter mingling with the dry rustle of wheatgrass. Buildings in various stages of completion rose like tentative promises, with hand-painted signs asking for hammers, hands, and hope.

Mary and Elizabeth strolled toward the main tent, skirts freshly laundered but boots still bearing yesterday's road. The scene ahead was almost pastoral in its industry, as if a church picnic had collided with a frontier hospital. Sarah, sleeves rolled and apron damp, spotted them and waved.

"Good morning, doctors," she called, her smile as easy as sun on the porch rail. "Did you sleep?"

Mary returned her smile. "Deeply. I might've slept

through the clinic if no one woke me."

Sarah chuckled. "That's why we rise early in the country—wait too long, and the day carries on without you."

They walked in step toward the tent.

"I'm all for sleep," Elizabeth said, rubbing her arms, "but since I'm vertical, I suppose I'll make myself useful."

Sarah nodded toward the swell of patients beyond the flap. "We're getting busier. Why don't you lend Dr. O'Brien a hand with the adults?"

With a nod, Elizabeth veered off toward the scrub station. Sarah reached into her apron and drew out a folded paper. "This came for you early this morning. Telegraph from Miss Brighty."

Mary took it, her fingers tingled, caught between fear and the ache of wanting. She read aloud: 'You are being sent north to the Battle River Prairie District right away'.

A breath caught in her throat. There it was—the line drawn between before and after. "I'm being placed," she whispered, then laughed, gripping Sarah's arm before catching herself. "Oh—sorry, I didn't mean—"

"It's wonderful news, Mary. Truly," Sarah said with a smile. "We're well covered here—for today, at least. Start thinking about the supplies you'll need. I'll review your list and add anything I think might be essential for the wilderness. We can telegraph it to Miss Brighty this afternoon."

Mary nodded, dazed, the words not yet settling into shape. So it was real. The fantasy she'd clung to through sleepless nights and bitter mornings had turned into an address.

"If you're sure I won't be missed."

"I'm sure. Go on, get started. You'll want to be ready."

She stepped away as though the ground beneath her had subtly shifted, and her body hadn't yet caught up. Excitement warred with a flicker of doubt—Was she ready? Was she enough? But the thought was brushed aside like a horsefly. She would be. She had to be.

She hesitated, a ripple of uncertainty threading through the moment. "Am I the only one with a posting?"

Sarah raised an eyebrow. "You asking about Elizabeth and Helen?"

Mary nodded, just as a sharp squeal of joy rang out from across the clinic.

"Well," Sarah said with a chuckle, "I guess they know."

The three women converged in the clearing, their voices a low, excited hum. They leaned close, laughing like conspirators.

"I can't believe it," Mary beamed. "Battle River Prairie! I want to leave today."

"I'm headed to the Peace River Area," Elizabeth said. "The last frontier, they say."

Helen's eyes widened. "High Level for me. They say it's remote. Lonely, maybe. But I suppose that's the point."

"I'll stay in Jarvie until Miss Brighty arrives," Mary said, still breathless. "She'll bring my luggage and equipment next week."

"We're with the clinic for another week," Helen added. "But then—we're off too. Perryvale tomorrow. It's our last stop before we part ways."

Their laughter came easy, but beneath it lay something quieter—a thinning thread of togetherness. Each word between them was weighted, each smile slightly too long.

Mary, sensing the drift, grinned. "Let's not turn into poets just yet. You've work to do, and I've a list to compile. But if this is our last night together, we'll feast properly. One more evening, all of us, under the same roof."

As the sun dipped behind the pines, casting long amber shadows across Jarvie, the clinic quieted. Inside Sarah's house, lanterns glowed and bread cooled on the sill. The table had been set with quiet care—wooden bowls, mismatched cutlery, a humble spread of stew, beans, and thick slices of buttered rye.

The women gathered, chairs scraping the floor, the weight of the day melting in the warmth of supper.

Elizabeth sipped from her cup. "Ah, that storm at sea. That ship pitched like it had a personal grudge."

Helen groaned. "You're lucky. I practically lived in the washroom."

Mary smiled into her bowl. "And yet, the ship had its charm. The piano music, the scent of cardamom, the ballroom's shimmer... all of it seems so far away now."

"And Quebec," Elizabeth added. "French at every turn. Remember that bakery near the cathedral?"

Mary nodded. "And now, here we are. From city streets to prairie dust."

Elizabeth raised an eyebrow. "Have you blocked out the mud already? I found grit in my teeth for days."

Their laughter, full-throated and unguarded, filled the small kitchen.

Helen lifted her glass. "To whatever comes next. May it be wild, and may we be ready."

They clinked their glasses gently, a toast not just to the future—but to the tether that had, however briefly, bound them here.

Later, in the hush that followed laughter, Mary lingered at the window. Outside, the wind threaded itself through wheat and fenceposts. She traced the rim of her cup, a knot of questions tightening in her chest. She had asked for this—this calling, this wilderness. But had she known what it would cost?

Behind her, the others laughed again, some small joke lost to the moment. She let it pass. For now, she would let herself feel everything—the joy, the ache, the unspoken hope that this path would lead not just onward, but inward.

CHAPTER 25

The next morning, with the sunrise casting a warm golden glow, Mary entered Sarah's home after her farewells to the traveling clinic and her friends. Sarah, already prepared for rounds, packed medical equipment into her bag.

"Did the doctors get out fine?" she asked, her gaze briefly shifting from the medical supplies to ensure she wasn't forgetting anything.

"Yes, they did. I'm going to miss those two," Mary said, her voice soft with the ache of departure. "We've been through a lot together."

Sarah handed her a medical bag. "Friendships are never forgotten. But it's time to move on. I got an urgent message—twenty miles out, a woman's been gored by a cow."

They stepped into the morning light and made their way to the waiting democrat. A single horse stood harnessed, stamping against the cool, waking earth.

As they climbed aboard, Mary took in the endlessness of the land. Hills rolled into distance like the swell of waves, broken only by the silhouettes of spruce and the stitch of distant fencing.

"It's so different from the city," she said, the words caught between awe and apprehension. "The openness, the quiet... it's almost overwhelming."

Sarah nodded, reins in hand. "Nature has its way of making you feel both small and connected. Out here, you're at its mercy."

The horse's hooves fell in rhythm with the hush of trees and bird call, a steady cadence that filled the long stretches between conversation. She pointed to a ridge ahead. "You see those hills? She lives just beyond them."

Mary squinted into the haze. "Quite a journey. Do you do this often?"

"More than you'd think. Folks out here rely on us. We're their lifeline."

As the trail narrowed and the ride grew rougher, she braced herself against the democrat's edge. Her knuckles whitened. Sarah gave a small laugh.

"Get used to these bumpy rides. Being a doctor in the wilderness means being ready for anything."

Mary glanced sideways. "Anything?"

"Unpredictable weather. Washed-out roads. Patients

hidden in valleys like secrets. And the wildlife. You'll learn their tracks before long."

Mary tried for a steady smile. "Wildlife? Like bears?"

"Bears, wolves, moose—you name it. But don't fret." Sarah reached behind the seat and retrieved a burlap sack. From it, she pulled a rifle. "We come prepared."

Mary fell quiet, absorbing the unspoken rule: out here, you carried what you feared.

The journey stretched beneath a sky that felt too big for words. Trees gave way to fields and fields to forest again. She stared into the wild and wondered what kind of doctor she would need to become to belong here.

By midday, they arrived at a small, weather-beaten shack. Inside, daylight filtered through thin curtains, drawing pale lines across a humble bed where Mrs. Watson lay. Her eldest daughter, barely fourteen, tended to her mother with a quiet that felt practiced.

She stepped inside and froze. Her breath caught.

The wound was brutal. The cow's horn had punctured beneath the breast, tearing flesh and confidence in one clean stroke.

"Oh my God—and no hospital," she whispered.

Her stomach tightened. This wasn't theory anymore. No antiseptic tiles. No clean linens. Just splintered floorboards and blood in the open air. For the first time, the word doctor felt less like a title and more like a promise she wasn't sure she could keep.

Sarah didn't hesitate. She set her bag down, opened it with precision. "Let's get to work."

Mary nodded, pulse ringing in her ears.

They moved without speaking, the way dancers do when the rhythm is survival. Mary fetched the sterilized water while Sarah examined the wound.

"Chloroform to ease the pain," Sarah murmured, applying it gently. Mary glanced at the meager supplies.

"I guess I won't be getting the ether I asked for," she muttered, a wry smile breaking the tension.

Sarah's eyes crinkled. "Sometimes humor's the best medicine—especially out here."

Mary forced a smile, but part of her hovered just above her hands, watching. She had learned to suture under white lights. This was older, more primitive. A strange calm settled over her as instinct took hold.

The daughter stepped back, wide-eyed. Mary offered her a reassuring look.

Together, they stitched and cleaned and bound. Time dissolved into gauze and breath.

The light dimmed, flickering with the kerosene lamp, its glow dancing across their focused expressions. The scent of blood mixed with pine and lamp oil, rooting the moment in something deeply physical, deeply real.

When it was over, Sarah wiped her brow and nodded. "We did good."

The air had shifted. Even the silence felt different—less fearful, more reverent.

Mary helped gather the tools, her hands trembling slightly. She held them tightly to still them. The box of thank-you gifts—homemade bread, dried apples, a wool shawl—felt like too much and not enough.

They stepped outside. The sun was already slanting westward, turning the sky to brass. As they loaded the supplies into the democrat, fatigue settled deep in Mary's bones.

Sarah climbed aboard and took the reins. "Well, that was quite successful. What did you think of your first case in the wilderness?"

Mary exhaled, long and slow. "It was more primitive than I expected. But I see now what the early doctors faced. And I see why they stayed."

The ride home was quiet, the land gilded in late light. Pine mingled with dust in the breeze, the world settling around them.

"You won't find modern conveniences out here," Sarah said, watching the trees blur past. "No electricity. No help five minutes away. But there's honesty in that."

Mary nodded. "I'm fine with that. It'll take time, but I think it's worth it."

She glanced at the gift box beside her.

"You'll get used to that," Sarah said. "Out here, money's scarce. But gratitude isn't. They'll pay in chickens, potatoes, firewood. I've had bannock cooked over coals and smoked fish wrapped in birch bark. It's a kind of wealth, really."

Mary let her hand rest atop the box. The sunset spilled gold over the hills, and the air cooled with night's slow arrival.

As Jarvie's first lamps glimmered on the horizon, she felt the day settle in her like silt. She had made it through. And though every part of her ached, there was something stronger beneath it: a rising, a readiness.

The democrat rattled down the last stretch of road. She leaned into the rhythm, letting the wilderness teach her how to stay upright—not just on the road, but in whatever came next.

CHAPTER 26

Under the high blush of a northern summer morning, Jarvie stirred quietly, sunlight spilling across fields where dew clung to grass like memory. Mary stood in the yard behind Sarah's home, pinning damp linens to the line—the rhythmic gesture oddly soothing. She had begun to settle into the town's slower pulse, letting herself be rocked by the simplicity of chores. But the steadiness of routine didn't last.

Sarah appeared with a pair of horses in tow—one saddled, one not.

"You up for a ride?" she called, her voice bright with mischief.

Mary wiped her hands on her skirt. "I was, until I saw the missing saddle."

"Oh, that?" Sarah waved a hand. "Most of your calls won't come with paved roads and stirrups. You'll need to know how to ride bareback. Sometimes you only get one horse, and no time to fuss."

Mary's gaze drifted to the unsaddled horse. Her body betrayed her—heart quickening, breath shallowing—as if it knew the stakes before she did.

"I've never... not without a saddle."

Sarah chuckled. "Then today's the day. Come on—it's easier than it looks."

Mary sighed. Well, she thought, I didn't come here to stay comfortable. She ducked inside to change, returning a few minutes later dressed in crisp English riding gear: jodhpurs, low boots, a fitted blazer, and her black cap. She looked every inch the part—of a different story entirely.

Sarah grinned. "Well, you certainly win points for style."

She smiled, adjusting her cap. "Don't be fooled. I'm as green as spring grass."

They led the horses into an open field. The bareback horse flicked its tail with idle amusement as Mary circled it, sizing up the animal like a problem with no clear solution.

She exhaled slowly, letting her palm rest briefly on the horse's flank. Let's not make a fool of ourselves today, she thought.

"Okay," she said aloud, staring at its height. "How on earth do I get on this thing?"

Sarah stepped forward. "Grab a handful of mane—left hand high, right near the withers. Swing that leg over like you mean it."

Mary nodded and reached for the mane. She braced herself, then leapt—

—and promptly fell flat on her back in the dirt.

The horse turned its head, peering down with what looked like mild amusement. Sarah bent double, laughing.

"Again," Mary muttered, brushing off her pride. "Just need more lift."

"Pull harder this time. Don't worry about the mane—he's tougher than he looks."

She counted down like a soldier at the breach, then hurled herself skyward.

Too much lift. She sailed over the horse and landed with a thud on the far side.

Sarah was gasping now, wiping tears from her eyes. "Okay, maybe something in between."

Mary shot her a mock glare. "Noted."

On the third attempt, she found her balance. She clung to the horse, heart hammering, trying to disguise her triumph as calm.

"Well done," Sarah said, genuinely impressed.

Mary stroked the horse's neck. "Thank you, thank you. You're a patient soul."

They set off at a walk, sunlight rippling through the poplars lining the trail. She shifted in discomfort.

"I could really use a saddle," she muttered, tugging at her jacket.

"Luxury of the south," Sarah quipped. "This is the northern way."

As they ambled beside the river, Mary gradually found her rhythm. Her muscles adjusted; the awkward stiffness gave way to something more intuitive. Smitty's breath moved beneath her like a bellows—steady, unbothered. Her hands, once clenched with fear, softened in his mane.

The land unfolded around them—wide, green, forgiving. And though her seat ached and her thighs burned, something in her began to loosen—her grip on control, perhaps. On perfection. On the polished self she'd brought across an ocean.

"What's his name?" she asked.

"Smitty. He knows what he's doing. Just hold on and trust him."

She leaned forward. "Good boy, Smitty. Let's try not to kill me today."

Moments later, the calm ruptured.

"Let's pick up the pace," Sarah called.

Mary gave a cautious squeeze with her legs—and Smitty responded with enthusiasm. Too much.

"Whoa! WHOA!" she yelled, clutching his mane as he surged forward.

The tighter her grip, the harder he flew—mistaking panic for command.

Sarah chased after, laughing through alarm. "Hold on, Mary!"

Smitty veered toward the barn, hooves drumming like hail. She held fast, teeth gritted, unsure whether to jump or pray.

He darted through the gate and swerved sharply. She slid forward, clung to his neck—and lost her grip. She tumbled, rolled through the dust—

—and landed squarely in a water trough.

With a tragic splash, it tipped.

Silence.

Then water cascaded over her, an ungodly baptism.

The sun caught the arc of water midair, and for a breathless second, it glittered like a veil.

Sarah skidded to her side. "Mary! Are you alright? Say something!"

She groaned, peeled mud from her eyes, and sat up.

"I think... I think I need a saddle."

Sarah collapsed in laughter.

Mary, drenched and sore, looked skyward. Despite herself, she smiled.

There'd been no training for this kind of medicine—no chapter on humility, no practiced response for failure. But maybe this, too, was preparation. Not the kind she'd envisioned, but the kind she'd need. A quiet unraveling. A shedding.

So this, then, was the wilderness's first lesson—not grace, but the grace to fail.

CHAPTER 27

The next day, Katie Brighty arrived in Jarvie beneath a sky the color of brass, the sunlight folding the town in a warm, honeyed hush. Her presence—efficient, exacting—cut through the quiet like a latch on a well-packed case clicking shut in morning air. She descended from the truck with her usual air of brisk capability, boots firm in the dust, eyes already scanning for Nurse Conlin.

Mary watched from the stoop as the familiar truck rolled to a stop, its bed groaning under crates and barrels, her own luggage among them. It smelled faintly of oil, sun-warmed pine, and anticipation.

"There you are, Nurse Conlin," Katie called, voice crisp but not unkind. "I've brought just about everything you ordered."

Sarah, sleeves rolled, surveyed the delivery with her usual sharp-eyed calm. "As always, your timing is unnervingly perfect."

Katie smiled. "And Mary, I haven't forgotten you. Luggage, equipment, notes from me, and a few little extras. Think of it as Christmas in June."

Mary grinned. "Do I get to shake the boxes first?"

"Only if you promise not to guess correctly."

While Sarah and Katie exchanged inventory lists and logistical shorthand, Mary let herself step back—just enough to absorb the small, bright rhythms of the scene: the scrape of crates on metal, the laughter of children skimming like birds across the street, the earthy scent of drying mud and spruce.

Sarah turned to the driver. "Once we've unloaded these, take the rest to the station. Make sure they're secured."

"Yes, ma'am," the driver replied, tipping his hat.

She waved over two local boys lingering by the fence. "Careful with those," she warned, eyeing the crate labeled Fragile. The boys nodded solemnly, pride stiffening their spines. Mary watched them—so earnest, so eager—and wondered what it must feel like to grow up with wilderness on all sides and the railway as your only escape.

They walked together toward Sarah's house, the three women shoulder to shoulder, their footsteps echoing against the low hum of the town. Mary glanced down at her packing list. "It's quite the load we're hauling."

"Twenty-nine crates," Katie said. "Over a thousand pounds. A small fortune in gauze and glass and good intentions."

Mary raised an eyebrow. "Any chance one of them contains a spare nurse?"

Katie smirked. "No, but there might be chocolate."

Inside, the house radiated the comforting clutter of a place lived in and well-loved. Sarah set about gathering water for washing up while the other two prepared a simple meal—bread, cured ham, boiled eggs, and stewed apples. The work was easy, companionable.

At the table, laughter found them quickly. Sarah poured strong tea into mismatched mugs and offered a final toast. "To Mary. May Battle River Prairie know how lucky it is."

Mary's throat tightened. "I'm the lucky one. I've had the best introduction a doctor could ask for."

Sarah set her mug down and crossed the room. She wrapped her in a hug that was all backbone and heart. "I was glad to have you. I wish we could keep working together."

Mary held on an extra beat. "Well, if ever you feel the urge to trek three hundred miles north, I'll put the kettle on."

Laughter softened the ache of goodbye. But it was

goodbye all the same.

The truck rumbled down the road toward the train station, the afternoon light catching on its windshield like a glinting coin. At the platform, townsfolk had gathered—Sarah among them, the boys too, their hair wind-whipped and eyes bright.

"Bye, Doc!" they called in unison.

Mary waved, a genuine smile breaking through the press of emotions. "Stay clear of the tracks, boys!"

She turned to Sarah, hugged her once more, and whispered, "Thank you. For everything."

"We'll meet again," she replied.

Then the train pulled forward, cutting cleanly through the edge of town.

Aboard, the compartment was plain but private. Katie lifted her satchel onto the upper bunk and sat with a sigh.

"You made quite an impression, Doctor Percy."

Mary gazed out the window, watching Jarvie shrink behind them. She had arrived a stranger with polished boots and trembling hands. Now she left with dust on her hem and something steadier in her chest.

"I had good people around me. Sarah's a marvel. I learned more from her than from any textbook."

Katie nodded. "That's why I sent you here first. Battle

River will challenge you. But you're ready."

Mary turned from the window, her voice quiet but certain. "I hope so. I want to be."

Katie raised an eyebrow. "Any regrets?"

She shook her head, then smiled. "Just one. I should've asked what was in the Christmas crates."

They laughed, and the train rattled on, pulling them into the green unknown. Beyond the glass, the landscape opened—pine, river, sky. And somewhere ahead, the place where Mary's next chapter would begin.

CHAPTER 28

They dined in the train's quiet elegance as the northern wilderness unfurled beside them. The carriage hummed with the measured cadence of wheels against rail, a sound that had become, in just a few days, the pulse of passage. Out the broad windows, the evening sun poured across the skin of Lesser Slave Lake, gilding the water and low brush in a light so tender it seemed to forgive everything it touched.

Mary sat back, her fork idle, eyes drinking in the scenery as if to memorize it. Behind her gaze, memories stirred—the manicured streets of Birmingham, the cool marble of her family's foyer, Cecile's quiet hands folding clean linens, the scent of violets on pressed collars. That life felt more imagined now than lived, a museum behind glass. Here, in the vast muscular silence of the North, her past looked small. Decorative.

"Quite a departure from what you're accustomed to,

isn't it?" Katie asked, not unkindly.

Mary smiled, a touch rueful. "It is. A world away from Birmingham. But... I feel something here. Something unspoken and immense. As though the land has a memory older than any I brought with me."

Katie nodded, eyes on the distance. "It does. And it remembers who tends it with care."

Mary turned her gaze back to the window, where dusk bled slowly into the shoulders of spruce and sky. She said, quietly, almost to herself, "It is beautiful. I'm looking forward to finally settling in."

Katie unfolded a napkin and dabbed at the corner of her mouth. "We'll reach Peace River Town soon. From there, we transfer the crates to the ferry landing. That'll give us a chance to meet with Dr. Sutherland at the Irene Cottage Hospital. He's the nearest physician to your post—first-rate surgeon, and solid in general practice. You'll like him."

"I can't wait," she said, her voice touched with earnest anticipation.

The waiter arrived to clear their plates. Porcelain clinked softly against silver, and the coffee came hot, aromatic, grounding. Katie leaned back in her seat and studied Mary a moment before speaking.

"No sense dancing around it," she said. "Life up there will demand more than most jobs. You'll be tending to three, maybe four hundred settlers. More coming every week. Most of them won't speak English as a first language. There'll be Metis families, too, and Cree. They'll be cautious at first. Rightly so. But once they trust you, they'll trust you fully."

She listened, hands folded in her lap, the weight of responsibility settling not as a burden but as a kind of promise.

"There's a trading post about four miles from your shack," Katie continued. "Joe Bissette and his wife Sally run it. Salt of the earth. They'll be your link to Edmonton and to me."

"And my new home?"

"The District Nurse's shack. It's yours now—a narrow place by the trail that'll soon be the new road north. Bridge construction is underway across the Battle River. Should be finished by the end of summer. You'll hear the hammering soon enough."

Mary's eyes lit with something fierce and bright. "It sounds... real. I know it won't be easy. I know I'll be alone. But the idea that I can be useful—really useful—that steadies me more than comfort ever could."

Katie's hand found hers on the table, a warm, brief pressure. "Mary, I knew the moment you walked into my office in Edmonton. You've got it. Whatever 'it' is. You'll make a difference."

They shared a quiet smile, the kind that didn't need words to hold its weight. Outside, the world kept changing. The trees grew taller, the rivers wider, the sky more open. The waiter poured the coffee, and steam rose in thin, fragrant ribbons. The train moved on, slipping into dusk. Shadows stretched across the land like long thoughts. And in the slow hush of that northern twilight, she leaned into the window and watched her future rise in silhouette against the vanishing light.

CHAPTER 29

Mary stepped down from the train into the heat-slicked air of Peace River Town, the station alive with movement and voices, all folded beneath the hum of midsummer. The platform baked beneath their boots. Above, the sky stretched hard and bright, scorched thin by the sun.

Katie moved with practiced ease, handing off baggage tags to a waiting livery attendant. Mary, ever mindful, leaned in. "Please—those crates are fragile. Especially the medical glass."

The attendant nodded, and Katie, catching the note of authority in her tone, smiled. "Don't worry. Each crate will be treated like the Crown Jewels."

Mary offered a half-laugh, brushing her sleeve as if to shake off the worry. "If only the King knew what we're carrying."

Their ride waited just beyond the station—an open-topped motor car that shimmered in the heat. They climbed in, skirts gathered, eyes scanning the wide unspooling of the town: the angled storefronts, the raw wood of new construction, the dusty trails where dogs slept under carts.

The Irene Cottage Hospital rose like a promise—a white clapboard haven shaded by cottonwoods. Its screened doors welcomed a breeze laced with lavender and the faint bite of carbolic. Inside, sunlight slanted across wooden floors, catching dust motes mid-air like suspended thoughts.

Nurse Ellen was finishing a dressing change when they entered. She looked up, eyes brightening with recognition. "Katie Brighty, just as I live and breathe." Then, turning to Mary, she extended a hand with a warm smile. "And you must be the new doctor."

Mary took her hand, her own smile sincere. "Yes—Dr. Mary Percy. It's a pleasure."

Katie gestured between them. "Mary, this is Nurse Ellen—one of my finest. Like Conlin, hand-picked for the North."

Ellen gestured them through a narrow hallway, walls painted a weary shade of blue. Photographs of staff and landscapes hung between doorways; some faded, others newly framed. The scent here was a careful balance—lavender over liniment, the sterile comfort of clean hands and stitched wounds.

They stepped into a courtyard bathed in light. There, on a bench worn smooth by weather and waiting, sat

Dr. Sutherland—coffee in one hand, cigarette in the other, shoulders loose with the rhythm of an earned pause.

He stood when he saw them. "Katie. I thought I heard the train." His voice was dry but genial, with that seasoned note of someone long used to bearing both welcome and bad news. "And you must be Dr. Percy."

"I am," she said, meeting his grip with her own.

"Come sit," he offered. "Coffee's strong, but we're out of sugar and cream. Northern hospitality at its finest."

She took the mug and sipped. A bitter jolt rippled across her tongue. She suppressed a grimace. "I hope this isn't a sign of what's to come," she joked.

He laughed. "It is. But you'll get used to it—or you'll learn to drink faster."

They talked there, beneath the hush of cottonwoods. He spoke candidly of the realities ahead—medical shortages, cultural barriers, the creeping spread of tuberculosis among the Metis and Cree, the influx of Polish and Ukrainian settlers. His words were plainspoken but steeped in respect.

She listened, absorbing not just facts, but the way he carried them. There was no armor in his tone—only fluency in hardship.

When she asked, "And how do you manage it all?" he answered simply: "By staying."

Nurse Ellen approached quietly. "Doctor, you're needed. It's the Red Elk boy."

Sutherland stood, brushing ash from his lapel. "No day's quiet for long." He turned to Mary, nodding. "We'll talk again. You'll do well."

He disappeared through the screen door, and she watched the mesh swing shut behind him like a breath held, then released.

Katie leaned in. "Well?"

Mary's voice came softer than expected. "He's rooted here. Not just working in the North—but of it. There's a depth in how he speaks of his patients... it's more than duty."

Katie nodded. "He's seen more than most. Learned how to listen. You'll want that kind of example."

The sun shifted, casting shadows that danced along the bench where moments ago they'd all sat. Mary turned her face to the light, her coffee cooling in her hand.

"I'm glad he's here," she said. "It helps—to know there's someone who understands the terrain, not just the geography but the lives threaded through it."

"And what about you?" Katie asked, watching her closely.

Mary looked to the horizon, where a haze of green

forest met sky. "I'm ready," she said. "Or I will be. I want to earn the right to be part of this place—not just visit it."

She lifted her mug in a quiet toast. "To beginnings. To bitter coffee and bold intentions."

And then, with a theatrical wince after another sip, she added, "And to never running out of sugar."

Katie laughed, the sound trailing on the wind like a promise not yet written.

CHAPTER 30

At approximately two o'clock in the afternoon, they descended the sun-warmed slope toward the riverfront, their boots finding rhythm in the dust. Before them, moored like a memory made solid, was the D.A. Thomas—its great paddlewheel at rest, gleaming in slices of light, as though still dreaming of coal and current. Originally built to haul industry out of the wilderness, it had since traded oil for elegance, and now bore passengers and provisions alike into the quiet heart of the North.

The foreshore pulsed with midsummer life. Students had fled their classrooms; families lined the edge of the wharf, waving handkerchiefs or balancing atop crates for a better view. The D.A. Thomas, with its fluted stacks and lacquered railings, held the attention of the town like a stage at curtain rise. Mary paused, letting the air fill her lungs—smoke from the boiler mingled with spruce and river weed, an earthy perfume that would become, she suspected, the scent of this chapter in her life.

She ran her gloved fingers along the rail, tracing time into wood. She imagined its past: firewood hauled aboard at midnight stops, fiddles playing under canvas, the slap of cards and laughter in the saloon. The ghosts of those nights moved with her as she boarded.

Their cabin was modest but trim, its window opening onto the river's slow gleam. She and Katie changed for the voyage. Mary slipped into a linen blouse and skirt, the creases still whispering of Edmonton. She glanced at herself in the mirror—a face wind-flushed, eyes sharpened by weeks of travel. There was a new stillness behind them, a readiness.

Back in the lounge, she stood at the window, hands wrapped loosely around the balustrade. Outside, the scene was choreography—dockhands calling to one another, crates trundled up ramps, a dog barking from the deck below. And there, just off-center, stood the Captain: tall, sun-aged, issuing commands with the easy authority of someone long accustomed to wind and water. Her gaze lingered, a flicker of curiosity threading through her composure.

She leaned her forehead lightly against the glass. The river was broad but intimate, close enough to reach the bank with a stone. Trees leaned in from the shoreline as though listening. It struck her—how narrow the space was between wilderness and water, between what she was and what she might become. Her breath fogged the glass briefly, a small cloud of presence. Was she still the same woman who had hesitated at the edge of Birmingham's polished corridors? Or someone else entirely?

"Arriving in the middle of the night," Katie murmured beside her, unsettling the quiet. "How will we even find our way? I do hope the teamster I hired stays put."

Mary turned, half-smiling. "You're making me nervous now. But... there's something about the unknown. It might be a story worth telling."

"Adventures are easier in daylight," Katie muttered, though the corner of her mouth betrayed her amusement.

They settled into the velvet seats, the lounge glowing with burnished mahogany and low brass lamps. A waiter swept by with clinking trays, and the murmur of passengers rose around them, layered with the soft clink of glass and the warm cadence of cutlery.

Katie requested to speak with the Captain, and soon a crewman approached. "He'll see you shortly," he said, then added, "We're now scheduled to leave closer to seven."

Mary looked back to the window, where the water caught the last clarity of the afternoon. Shadows had begun to stretch and soften, folding the shoreline in gold.

She thought of the places behind her—hospitals, city streets, voices clipped by civility. This place had none of that polish. But here, the roughness gleamed differently. It asked not who she had been, but whether she would stay.

"Let's embrace whatever comes," she said quietly. "Even a midnight landing. It might mark the beginning of something better than we imagined."

She didn't add what stirred beneath: a quiet flutter of nerves, not of fear, but of arrival. The world was not just opening, it was beginning to speak. And somewhere, something was waiting to meet her. Not destiny, perhaps. But something with hands weathered like oars, and a voice low as the current beneath the hull.

CHAPTER 31

The dining saloon of the D.A. Thomas wore its history like polish—dimly lit, hushed, the air thick with the quiet rituals of evening. Along the river's slow pull toward Fort Vermilion, the great paddlewheel murmured beneath them like a heartbeat. Mary and Katie sat at a table covered in white linen, the soft gleam of brass lamps casting warm halos over polished cutlery and fine china. The air smelled of roast duck, pipe smoke, and something subtler—perhaps nostalgia.

Nearby, the Anglican parson, Mr. Lamberton, murmured grace over his plate with a reverence born of habit. Two tables away, fur traders Sheridan Lawrence and Frank Jackson conversed in the cadences of old friends, laughter clipped short by the decorum of the setting. Mary was conscious of Frank's gaze, not intrusive, but quietly attentive. When their eyes met, something passed between them—not flirtation exactly, but the beginning of a question neither had yet asked. She was surprised by how it steadied her. It had been weeks of movement, of arrival and departure, and yet in that glance—brief as it was—she felt acknowledged in a way that reminded her of home. Or something better than home: belonging, without expectation.

The Captain approached with the gait of a man whose balance had long been shaped by current and keel. "Ladies," he said with a courteous dip of his head, gesturing to the empty chair beside them.

Katie nodded, shifting slightly in her seat. Her voice, when it came, was measured but earnest. She spoke of the late arrival of the hired teamster who might not wait through the dark. Her words were etched with the worry of someone trying not to show too much of it.

The Captain listened with the kind of patience only river men possess. "The Peace follows no clock but its own," he said. "We aim for nightfall, but truth be told, our arrival may drift closer to dawn."

Mary tilted her head. "So there's no fixed disembarkation?"

He smiled, eyes crinkling. "Several stops lie ahead, yes. But the river has its own sense of timing. We follow her lead."

As he departed, Katie leaned in, dryly murmuring, "That was as clear as river mud."

Mary chuckled. "Clarity's a city habit. Up here, I

suspect we trade it for trust."

After dinner, the Captain returned briefly to explain the hazards of night navigation—the driftwood deadheads, the sandbanks that moved like ghosts. But he reassured them: the teamster would wait. Those who lived by the river knew its moods well.

"No need to apologize," Mary said softly to Katie. "This ambiguity... it has its own kind of allure." Not long ago, she might have bristled at such vagueness. But something in her had shifted. Out here, certainty felt brittle; it cracked too easily. The unknown, though—it bent, it breathed. Maybe she could, too.

The dining saloon faded into laughter and porcelain clinks. She caught Frank watching her again, this time across the candlelight. She didn't look away. This time, she returned his look more fully, offering a smile that reached past politeness. There was something in his steadiness that intrigued her—not just the strength of his frame, but the way he seemed to belong to this place.

By nightfall, the ship was anchored. A crewman informed them they'd be first off in the morning. When they retired to their berths, the river lulled them with the soft shush of current against the hull.

But dawn came late. By the time they rose, the D.A. Thomas was still pushing upriver, the world outside their window wrapped in fog and possibility. Mary, tousled and eager, wandered into the breakfast hall, following the promise of coffee with the devotion of a pilgrim. The dining room, plainer by daylight, held its own honest charm—sunlight catching on windows, and the aroma of eggs and coffee washing over them like grace.

By eight-thirty, land approached. The river widened and then narrowed again, drawing its passengers toward something still unseen. Gulls wheeled above as though announcing their arrival.

On deck, they stood ready. She watched the landing draw near—the planked dock, the tall grass beyond, and the solitary figure of a teamster waiting beside a cart stacked high with hay.

"Seems we have our escort," she said.

"Our next adventure," Katie replied, her tone lighter now.

The gangplank dropped with a thud. A moment later, they were on solid ground, the deckhands lowering their crates with practiced care. The teamster, face lined like a map of the territory, tipped his hat. "Ladies. This all your kit?"

"All of it," Katie replied. "You sure you're ready for the haul?"

He laughed, low and musical. "Load's lighter than a dry sermon. We'll be fine."

But as they studied the wagon—narrow, weathered,

piled high—Mary hesitated. It looked like something patched together with stories and splinters. Would it hold everything she brought—and everything she hadn't yet named? Then came the sound of boots on planks. Frank and Sheridan approached, sleeves rolled, hands calloused, eyes kind.

"That wagon might protest," Mary said, half-joking.

Frank stepped forward. "We're heading that way. Let us help."

She opened her mouth to decline, but he continued easily, as if they'd already agreed. "Besides, word is you're here to help us. Seems fair we do the same."

He introduced himself and Sheridan. Mary offered her name in return, her voice steadier than she felt. Something in his presence pulled at her—a quiet gravity.

When all was loaded, he gestured toward the cart. "After you, Doctor."

The title still landed oddly in her ears. Not unwanted, just... new. Like a coat she hadn't quite worn in. She placed a hand on the cart's edge, felt the warmth of sun-soaked wood, and climbed up—awkwardly, but without hesitation. The boards creaked beneath her weight, her heart thrumming with a quiet, unfamiliar rhythm.

As they pulled away, the D.A. Thomas gave a final whistle, parting the morning air with its note of farewell. She turned to watch it shrink behind them, a white sliver on the moving blue.

Whatever waited ahead, she would meet it not as a visitor, but as someone willing to put her roots in unfamiliar soil.

CHAPTER 32

Under the relentless midday sun, the trail stretched ahead like a challenge issued by the land itself. The wagon, heavily laden, creaked and groaned as it approached an unforgiving hill. Frank, scanning the slope, rested his hand on the horse's flank and said, "Sorry, ladies, but I think it's best to lighten the load a bit and give the horses a break for this climb."

Mary stretched her limbs with a sigh of relief. Her joints ached, her back pinched. "Of course," she said, voice cheerful though her body protested. "A little walk might do us all good."

He extended a hand to help her down, and she took it. But her foot caught, and she tumbled—undignified and startled—into his waiting arms.

"It's all right. I've got you," he said, steady as stone.

She found herself wrapped in warmth and cedar-smelling wool. Her breath caught, not from fear but surprise, the physical closeness briefly disarming her. "Thank you," she said, quietly, blinking up at him. Something stirred—not quite romance, not yet—but the unexpected comfort of someone capable.

Katie glanced at her own shoes with doubt. "I hope these hold up for a hill climb."

He helped her down next with equal courtesy. "Let's hope you're spared the same entrance," he quipped.

She laughed. "Thank you, Frank. I'm glad my shoes didn't lead to an encore of Mary's adventure."

He encouraged the teamster to ease the horses forward. The wagon moved with effort, a reluctant beast on the slope. Mary walked behind, boots raising puffs of dust, sweat collecting at the back of her neck. Her arms ached from the earlier ride. This—this was the North. Not stories, not scenery, but strain. Grit.

"We'll need to lighten it more," Frank called, inspecting the incline. "The horses won't make it."

Katie groaned. "You mean we carry it?"

He gave her a sympathetic shrug. "Unless you want to make this hill your new home."

"I don't have the right clothes for this," she muttered.

Mary hesitated. She was still in a dress—lace collar wilting with sweat. "I've got something in the wagon we can change into," she offered. "Come on, Katie. Let's make it an adventure."

They changed behind the wagon, out of view, exchanging boots and skirts for trousers and cotton shirts. Mary rolled her sleeves with more conviction than confidence.

"Better?" Katie asked.

"Not exactly fashionable," Mary replied, "but I'll trade style for solid footing."

Frank selected a few crates. "We'll take these first. Essentials only."

Under the hot sun, they each grabbed suitcases and tucked awkward bundles under their arms. Mary felt the weight not just in her muscles but in her pride. She had never worked like this—not with her body.

She climbed. Thighs burned. Each step stole resolve.

Her dress had been a disguise. It had let her believe she could live here as she had in Birmingham. But the North didn't allow for illusions. Each step up the hill was a lesson: in humility, in physical reality, in the steep terrain of change.

Katie, cheeks flushed, laughed through her breathlessness. "This is a far cry from the city."

Frank, hauling a crate behind them, nodded. "Every day's an adventure up here."

They pressed on. The hill wasn't just a rise in the land—it became a test. Mary's boots slipped once, twice, but she steadied herself. At the top, sweat plastered her hair to her temples. Her chest rose and fell in ragged rhythm.

The wagon crested behind them, the horses finally free of their burden. Frank met them at the top. "Nicely done. No hill too steep for you two."

Mary met his gaze, exhausted but victorious. "We do what we must, Mr. Jackson."

Katie laughed. "What's a few more crates?" Her voice was different now—less hesitant, more rooted.

He handed each of them a handkerchief. Mary took it, wiping sweat from her brow. She was parched to her bones.

"Excuse me?" she called to the teamster. "Is there any water here?"

He spat, then held up two fingers and pointed ahead.

She glanced at Katie. "Two miles? Two minutes?"

"I hope for minutes," she said, breathless.

The wagon was reloaded. They walked behind it now, giving the horses rest. The heat radiated off the ground, the hum of mosquitoes ever-present.

Mary squinted toward the horizon. "Is there water

anywhere?"

The teamster nodded. "Small creek ahead. Half a mile. We'll stop for lunch."

The promise of water sharpened their focus. When they reached the creek, it was muddy and shallow.

Mary stared. "Are you kidding? That's it?"

Sheridan shrugged. "That's it. You won't find better between Peace River and Battle River Prairie."

She crouched beside the flow, assessing. The doctor in her knew better than to trust appearances. She filtered the water through a handkerchief, boiled it over a spirit stove, and poured it into their tin mugs with practiced precision.

Frank watched her—this woman who had arrived in a dress and now crouched in trousers beside a muddy creek, coaxing safety from the wild. He didn't speak, but something shifted in the way he looked at her.

"Well," she said, holding out the cup, "good thing I came prepared."

He took it with quiet reverence. The water steamed between them, fragrant with heat and something more difficult to name.

In that moment, she didn't feel tired. She felt capable.

She wasn't just traveling north.

She was becoming part of it.

Not just surviving it—but slowly earning her place in it.

CHAPTER 33

The northern evening unfurled its deceptive charm, twilight stretched thin and luminous across the wilderness, casting long violet shadows over the land. Eleven hours to travel eighteen miles: the North had its own way of marking time. Mostly on foot, sparing the horses where they could, they now stood before Mary's new home—a squat shack of timber and tar paper hunched beneath a stand of black spruce.

She stepped from the wagon with a weariness that went beyond the body. Her fingers, cracked and sore, curled around the doorknob. It was cool against the heat still lingering in her skin, indifferent to the long road behind her.

"It's locked?" she said. The disbelief in her voice frayed into fatigue. "In the middle of nowhere—who locks a door?"

Frank tried the knob. Then Sheridan. Nothing—like

the door was laughing behind its seams. She knocked hard, as if the door might apologize and swing open. Nothing.

"Well," Frank said, his tone edged with a dry sympathy, "that's well and truly locked."

She leaned her forehead against the wood, heat still rising off it from the day's sun. She felt herself unraveling, thread by thread. A grunt behind her: the teamster jerked his chin toward the river. There, faint in the dusk, a campfire flickered.

Frank straightened. "I'll go ask if anyone there has a key."

Mary swatted at a mosquito on her cheek. "Not without me. I'm not staying here to be eaten alive."

He laughed—low, warm. "Can't have you turning into mosquito dinner."

"We'll all go," he said, taking charge with that easy confidence she was beginning to rely on. "Sheridan, unload the wagon with the teamster. Miss Brighty, Dr. Percy—this way."

The fire beckoned through the trees. Lanterns in hand, they made their way through underbrush until voices and smoke came clearer. Men gathered in a loose circle, mugs in hand, silhouettes haloed by firelight.

"Evening," Frank called out. "Frank Jackson. This is Miss Brighty and Dr. Mary Percy. She'll be staying in the shack up the rise—only it's locked."

One man stood. Broad-shouldered, sun-split hands. "Hank Garrison. Foreman. Joe Bissette should have the key. Bill," he called over his shoulder, "go fetch it."

Katie added, "Tell Mr. Bissette I'll be by in the morning."

Hank gestured to logs by the fire. "Make yourselves at home. Cook's got coffee on."

The fire cracked, welcoming them in. Its warmth worked against the chill now bleeding through her sleeves. Mary folded herself onto a log, knees stiff, fingers aching from the day. Coffee. She could have wept for it.

"Any cream?" she asked.

Hank chuckled. "We take it black. Unless you prefer whiskey."

"Anything but black," she said, too tired to protest.

Cook poured steaming mugs. The aroma filled the camp: bitter, rich, slightly scorched. A splash of whiskey warmed it. She sipped, grateful for the burn.

"I'll help finish unloading," Frank said, rising. "We'll have you inside in no time."

Mary rose too, brushing dust from her trousers. She met his gaze, her thanks unspoken but full.

"You don't have to do all this," she said.

He placed a hand gently on her shoulder, warm through the thin fabric. She didn't lean into it—but she didn't step away either. "I want to. Get warm. I'll be back."

Their eyes held for a breath. The fire crackled behind her, but it was his touch that lingered.

She returned to her seat, cradling the mug between sore palms. The coffee was strong, smoky. The whiskey, subtle but real. She stared into the flames, letting the flicker match the flicker within her—a slow ignition. Gratitude. Hope. Something harder to name.

Maybe it was the whiskey.

Or maybe it was Frank Jackson, and the way he stepped forward, without being asked.

The shack would open. She knew that now.

And when it did, she would step inside—not just as the new doctor, but as someone beginning, quietly, to belong.

CHAPTER 34

In the quiet solitude of her shack, the morning sun filtered through the curtain-less window, a soft invitation to rise. Mary stirred beneath a blanket still askew from the night before, the same clothes clinging to her as yesterday's grit. The room, modest in its offerings, revealed itself slowly—an old bureau, a single chair, a few wall hooks. A table stood nearby, like a witness to her new life beginning.

The adjoining room, lit by a small window, was scattered with wood and rough edges. The kitchen and living space held three mismatched chairs, a narrow table beside a wood stove, and a sagging sofa where Katie still slumbered. Cozy, perhaps, if squinting with optimism.

She sat up slowly. Her back ached, but she welcomed the sensation—it meant she'd arrived. A glance toward the door caught the dry mud on the floor, yesterday's journey etched across the boards. Katie blinked groggily awake.

"Good morning," she offered.

"Just after eight," Mary said, checking her pocket watch. "We need to get moving if we want this place to feel like home before winter. Coffee?"

"Please."

Outside, the crates waited like unopened letters. Mary rifled through them, murmuring to herself, locating the spirit stove, kettle, and just enough determination to begin. Inside, Katie combed her hair and adjusted her collar, already looking more awake.

"I'll visit Mr. Bissette. Might bring him back to catch you up," Katie said, pausing with a smirk. "But first—I need a good kick in the pants. You did say coffee, didn't you?"

Mary grinned. "On its way."

Once Katie left, Mary surveyed the room. It was... tired. Dirt hung in the corners, crates loomed like judgmental relatives, and the air was thick with dust. She tied back her hair, rolled up her sleeves, and attacked it.

A broom, a bucket, and a borrowed resolve. She opened the windows, let the bugs stay out and the air in. Her arms burned as she scrubbed. Mud turned to foam, foam to rinse, and rinse to shine. She stepped back. Floors gleamed. Crates aligned. A small order carved from wilderness.

Then she caught her reflection—smudged face, streaked shirt, and hair somewhere between windswept and war-torn. She grabbed a towel, soap, and a washcloth, and headed for the river.

The sun warmed the crown of her head as she stood knee-deep in the current. Two flat rocks steadied her. She washed methodically: face first, then arms, then hair, the water cold and forgiving.

A sound rose above the river's hush—laughter. Male, echoing. She lifted her head, startled. Nothing visible. She resumed.

Then it came again, closer. She crept along the rocks, gazing upstream. There—about a hundred and fifty yards off—six men from the bridge crew, waist-deep and grinning, washing themselves and their clothes in the river like boys at summer camp. Their muscles caught the sun like sculpture, shoulders gleaming where water met light.

She paused, caught somewhere between amusement and a flicker of fascination. Then her foot betrayed her.

One misstep. A sharp slip. With a squeal more startled than fearful, she plunged into the river, limbs flailing. The cold slapped her. When she surfaced, soaked and sputtering, the laughter had shifted—closer now, directed squarely at her.

She rose, water clinging like accusation. The men,

now aware of their observer, turned, grinning like boys caught mid-prank, riverlight slick on their shoulders. On the bank stood Katie—and five others—including Joe Bissette.

Drenched, mortified, and caught red-handed.

Joe's smile was gentle, with a flicker of mischief. "You must be Dr. Percy."

Mary, breathless, managed, "Yes. How do you do?"

Katie stepped in, unbothered. "This is Mr. Bissette, the storekeeper."

He extended a hand. "Welcome to our corner of the North, Doctor. A spirited introduction, I must say."

Back at the shack, with Katie's arm around her, Mary mumbled, "I was just… bathing."

"Sure you were," she said, barely hiding a smirk.

Mary turned, cheeks flushed, and addressed the group. "Not exactly the introduction I imagined. Please, give me a moment to change—then we can pretend I arrived with more dignity."

Her sheepish wit melted any lingering awkwardness. The men chuckled, hats tipped, and the incident became story fodder by afternoon.

Later, the group gathered inside. She offered a drink—realized she had none—then laughed at herself. "Apologies. It's been a busy morning."

Joe waved it off. "We came with plans, not for refreshments."

Katie smiled. "They're here to help you settle in."

He added, "We've organized firewood, water, and a horse for your rounds. Even collected enough for the best saddle this town's seen."

She beamed. "I don't know what to say. Thank you—it's more than I imagined."

Mr. Hawthorne stepped forward. "We'd also like to fix up this place. Shingled siding for warmth. Cupboards in both rooms—one for your practice. And a cellar, with a proper well out back."

She could hardly speak. "That... would be extraordinary."

The others chimed in, brimming with plans. She watched, astonished. These strangers—already not strangers—were building her more than a home. They were laying the timbers of belonging.

As they left, Joe turned. "There's a dance Friday. Schoolhouse. I'll come by at eight, in my car."

"In your car?" she asked, startled.

"Drive it up to the new bridge. You'll cross the planks. I'll be waiting."

Katie, watching the exchange, raised an eyebrow.

After they departed, Mary stood in the doorway, stunned.

"I can't believe that all just happened," she said.

Katie grinned. "I might have told them they'd need to treat you like gold if they wanted you to stay."

She laughed, tears threatening. "I don't deserve you."

Katie lifted a hidden flask. "Minister Hoadley's finest. Shall we toast our last night?"

As dusk settled, they passed the whiskey and sketched their new lives by lamplight. Come morning, Katie's wagon stood ready.

Their hug was long, their silence longer.

"Promise me you'll write," Katie whispered.

"I promise."

And with that, she was gone.

She stood in the silence that followed, a weight in her chest she hadn't expected to carry so soon.

Mary watched the dust trail vanish. She turned, eyes damp but heart full. The dance loomed ahead. Her shack, her practice, her new place in the world.

She smiled to herself. If the North was full of secrets, perhaps this time, she was meant to be one of them.

CHAPTER 35

In the soft embrace of a summer night, she stood in her bedroom, filled with anticipation and the faint scent of wildflowers drifting through the open window. The room, modest in its furnishings, held a quiet charm she'd nurtured with care. Draped curtains lent grace. A worn rug brought warmth. The cushioned chair in the corner, where she'd once collapsed in doubt, now looked like it might hold a dream.

She opened her wardrobe—such as it was—and stared. The upcoming dance posed a dilemma. Dress down to match the schoolhouse and dirt floors? Or wear something beautiful, simply because she could?

She chose the gown.

It was the one indulgence she'd allowed herself before sailing—full-length, ocean-grey, with a softness that brushed against memory. She hadn't worn it since that farewell dinner in Birmingham, back when she believed a woman might practice medicine and keep hold of elegance.

She fastened the pearl-drop earrings—another relic—and gazed at her reflection. A woman poised between two worlds looked back. The gown whispered of civility, of ballroom floors and evenings with candlelight. Her face told another story. Wind-chapped. Firm. Slightly thinner.

"Is this the last time?" she whispered to the woman in the mirror. "The last time I wear anything like this?"

She didn't have the answer. She just smoothed the shawl over her shoulders and stepped into the night.

Outside, the shack stood sturdier now. Fresh shingles. A firebreak. The smell of turned earth from the waiting garden. Proof she wasn't just passing through.

The unfinished bridge rose ahead, a skeleton of timbers cast in silver by the moon. Two planks stretched across, laid thoughtfully—but not reassuringly. The river hissed below like it knew secrets.

She eyed her shoes. "Brilliant," she muttered. "A trail fit for a moose and I come dressed like a Brontë heroine."

She lifted her hem and stepped on.

The wood groaned beneath her feet. She paused.

Breathed.

One step.

Then another.

Halfway across, a plank shifted with a crack. Her foot slipped. She pitched forward, arms flailing—

Her fingers caught a support beam.

Heart pounding, she froze. One shoe hung half off. Her shawl nearly tumbled into the current. The moon stared down, unimpressed.

She clung there, breath shallow. The river roared beneath her like laughter.

'You could go back.'

But something in her stiffened. 'No.'

Not after what she'd crossed to get here—not the bridge, but the world itself.

She adjusted her shawl. Straightened her back.

Then, step by step, she made her way across.

At the edge of the clearing, a car idled, headlights haloing the brush.

"Need a lift?" Joe Bissette called, grinning from the driver's seat.

She laughed—short, relieved, a little wild. "More than you know."

She lifted her skirt and crossed the last few yards. Before she got in, she looked back once.

Her home stood in the moonlight, no longer just shelter but something that seemed, suddenly, to recognize her.

She touched the car door handle, thinking not just of the dance ahead, but of the woman she'd once been, and the one who'd walked a narrow plank to get here.

She smiled. Then stepped inside.

CHAPTER 36

Beneath the last flush of evening light, the sky blushed in tones of rose and gold as Joe Bissette guided his car along the dirt road, its tires humming with quiet purpose. She sat in the backseat, her hem lifted just enough to spare the dust, while Sally, poised beside her husband, narrated the journey with the grace of someone who had long since claimed this country as her own. Their glances—tender, practiced, true—spoke of nineteen years wound together like braided rope, tested and enduring.

As the schoolhouse came into view, a handful of locals were still stringing paper lanterns and garlands of pine. The building, modest and square, sat like a hopeful outpost on the edge of the prairie. Joe eased the car to a stop. "We're a bit early," he admitted with a grin. "But I wanted to take the scenic route. Show you the countryside at its gentlest."

Mary smiled. "It's beautiful. Thank you."

Sally lifted her casserole dish. "Come on, Mary. Time to meet the good folk of Battle River Prairie."

Inside, the schoolhouse pulsed with a gentle expectancy. Streamers hung like prayers, and the air buzzed with fiddle-tuning, pine sap, and molasses cookies. Sally ushered her toward the potluck table where neighbors gathered—Mr. and Mrs. Hawthorne, hands still dirt-stained from their fields; Clara Thompson, the schoolteacher, eyes bright behind wire-rimmed glasses.

"Welcome to Battle River," Clara said, shaking her hand with a grip surprisingly firm. "We're always grateful for another mind, especially one with a medical degree."

They fell into conversation about the school—how it bent around harvests and spring melts, how Indigenous children still hovered on the periphery. "We're trying," Clara said, her voice softening. "But the barriers are real."

"So is the need," Mary said. "Inclusion must begin somewhere."

Joe returned with spruce tea and a plate of bannock, slipping easily into their orbit. The tea was unexpectedly fragrant, with an edge of resin that reminded her of walking through pine groves as a child. "It's strange and wonderful," she admitted. "Like the place itself."

The fiddlers—Mr. and Mrs. Fife—struck up a tune that trembled with earnest joy. Couples rose. Laughter followed. Boots clomped. Skirts twirled. Mary accepted Joe's hand for a dance and found herself swept into a rhythm older than language.

She caught glimpses of herself—laughing, gliding, shedding hesitations like a shawl slipping off her shoulders. Her gown, too fine for this floor, caught the lantern light just the same.

Then, the music paused. She stepped aside, sipping tea as her gaze drifted.

Frank Jackson entered.

He wore a jacket that tried too hard not to matter, slacks that still bore the crease of effort. His boots were scuffed. He looked both ready and out of place, like someone still learning how to arrive. When their eyes met, something unspoken moved between them —recognition, perhaps, or a challenge.

"Mr. Jackson," she said as he approached, the syllables steadier than she felt.

"Dr. Percy," he replied, removing his hat. "I wasn't sure

you'd brave the bridge."

She lifted an eyebrow. "I wore the wrong shoes. But I got here."

He chuckled, low and warm. "Sounds about right."

They stood for a moment, side by side, watching the dance swirl around them.

"How's the shack?" he asked.

"Shingled. Cupboarded. Soon to be horsed," she said.

His grin widened. "Then you've already done better than most."

Their conversation wound gently—half banter, half curiosity. She teased. He returned it in kind. When he offered to fetch her another tea, she let him, surprised at the flicker of disappointment she felt as he stepped away.

From the window, she watched the moon rise above the pines. She remembered the sound of a waltz once played in a drawing room, the hush of a Birmingham evening pressing in. This was different. Wilder. Better, maybe.

Sally appeared beside her like a thought spoken aloud. "Frank's a good man," she said.

"He's lost someone."

"Louise. His wife."

Mary nodded slowly. "I didn't know."
"He doesn't talk about it. But she's there. Every time he comes home from Edmonton and sees the house is still quiet."

She folded that into herself. She would not pity him. But she would remember it.

When he returned, she met him with a smile that held both knowing and grace.

Joe and Frank spoke for a few minutes more, catching up, and then Joe clapped a hand to Frank's shoulder. "Come on, I want to show you the new shed we built out back. Shouldn't take a minute."

He glanced back at Mary, then nodded. "Excuse me, ladies. I'm being summoned."

"Of course," she said. "Don't be long. The tea's getting cold."

She turned toward the open window again, allowing the music and laughter to filter through her, softer now. The warmth of the gathering, the unexpected ease of conversation—it all shimmered in her like riverlight. And yet she felt the undertow too: a pull toward something quieter, something she hadn't named yet.

Sally leaned in. "I saw the way he looked at you."

Mary didn't reply. She didn't have the language yet. When the men returned, she met Frank's smile with one of her own.

"So? Did it meet your engineering standards?"

He laughed. "Let's just say I'm glad it's not holding up the roof."

Their laughter braided into the music, the light, the night.

Somewhere between one dance and the next, she felt the thread of her past tug gently. But she didn't look back. Not tonight.

Tonight, she danced.

And stayed.

CHAPTER 37

Amid the pulse of fiddle music and bootsteps, she found herself momentarily stilled, standing with Frank just beyond the thrum of the schoolhouse floor. Joe and Sally spun through a reel, their laughter rising like a familiar hymn. She envied how easy they made it look—decades of history collapsed into three steps and a turn. Around her, life danced. And yet—Something in her lingered.

You seem a bit lost in thought," he said, his voice gentle enough to bridge whatever distance he sensed forming.

She turned to him, meeting his gaze with a smile that barely brushed the surface. "Yes. Just taking it all in. The music. The company."

But beneath the pleasantry, her mind moved differently. The evening had surprised her—its warmth, its welcome, its unexpected intimacy. Frank, most of all. She hadn't anticipated this quiet gravity, the way his eyes seemed to read hers without intrusion.

"It's a beautiful night," he said, as if offering the moment back to her. "These dances don't happen often, but when they do, it reminds you what it means to belong."

She nodded, feeling the truth in it. Belonging. The word felt tentative on her tongue, like something borrowed. "It's a change of pace," she murmured. "And a beautiful one."

He studied her for a beat longer, then gently, "So what brought you here? Battle River's not exactly on the way to anywhere."

Her laugh came easily, carried on the wings of memory. "Not by accident, no. I needed a new beginning. And I thought—maybe out here, the ground would be quieter. More honest."

He nodded, slow. "A fresh start. I know the shape of that."

She looked at him then, properly, letting the silence stretch. "You lost someone."

"Louise," he said, the name a thread between them. "It's been a few years. She was the kind who made a room steadier just by being in it."

Mary felt the ache of it settle in her chest. Not pity. Recognition.

"I'm sorry. That kind of love doesn't end. It only

changes shape."

He nodded, and something softened in him. "She gave me two sons. That's what I hold onto."

She hesitated, then offered: "I never married. Medicine left little room. But I don't think I ever stopped wanting something real."

He glanced at her hands, pale in the lantern light. "Well. You made it here. That counts."

She smiled, wry. "And tonight, I danced. That's something too."

The heat of the room pressed closer. He noticed her flush before she did. "Would you like to step outside?"

She nodded. "Yes."

The night opened around them like a held breath. Crickets sang low in the grass. Stars flickered in a dome of ink.

When she shivered, he shrugged off his jacket and draped it over her shoulders. It smelled of pine and leather, worn through with something clean.

"Thank you," she said.

"Glad to be useful."

They walked in silence to the edge of the clearing, where the land fell away to the low trees and the sky unfolded entirely. Then, without warning, the heavens shimmered.

The Northern Lights.

A river of green and violet spilled across the sky, weaving between constellations like some ancient script.

She drew in a breath, her fingers unconsciously reaching. "Is this real?"

"As real as anything," he said, watching her more than the sky.

She stood in stillness, awed. "I've read about them. But to see them like this—it's..."

"Magic?"

"Yes. And no. Something deeper. Older."

They stood shoulder to shoulder, the silence between them rich with unspoken things. Then, as the wind shifted and she pulled the jacket closer, he gently placed an arm around her.

She didn't flinch. Didn't lean away. Instead, she guided his hand back when he hesitated, anchoring it with her own.

He looked down. "You're sure?"

Her voice was barely a whisper. "Yes."

She turned to him, her face lit by the dancing light. "Tonight has been full of things I didn't expect. The music. The sky. You."

His breath caught. "Me?"

She took his hands in hers. "You make it feel like there's room for something I thought I'd forgotten how to want."

For a moment, he couldn't answer. Then, simply: "That goes both ways."

They stood like that a while longer, two figures beneath a sky on fire, the night thick with promise.

When he finally offered her a ride, she declined with a smile. "I'm staying with the Bissettes tonight. But thank you."

He nodded, though his eyes lingered. "Goodnight, Mary Percy."

"Goodnight, Frank Jackson."

He took her hand and pressed a kiss to it, then walked into the dark. She watched until he disappeared among the trees, the aurora shifting silently above.

Back inside, the dance wound down. Laughter still echoed, but her world had grown quieter.

She had come for a beginning.

Perhaps tonight, she'd found it.

CHAPTER 38

On a radiant summer morning, the sun enveloped her modest home in a golden warmth, the scent of wildflowers drifting in through open windows. The little house, sturdy and spare, sat on the road north like a sentinel, quietly watching the world arrive.

Seven cars in a single day was a spectacle. That stretch of northern Alberta road was, in 1929, a vein through which hope and hardship pulsed. Land-seekers passed with wagons creaking under stoves, trunks, bedsteads, and dreams. Homesteaders—Norwegians, Germans, Hungarians, Ukrainians, Americans—brought with them clattering possessions and tired dogs that trotted faithfully behind. Some pushed north for promise. Others fled the south's despair.

She watched it all: the haphazard architecture of need—canvas tents, one-room shacks thrown up in a weekend. A father building while his child coughed in the tent beside him. Women weathered into strength, like Mrs. Robertson, who had bushwhacked her way here half a decade earlier. She listened to the land's quiet stories through their footsteps, their laughter, the clang of hammers on borrowed nails.

Inside these raw beginnings, she was a guest—eating pickled herring with Norwegians, beets with Russians, thick black bread with Germans. In one home, she spent seven hours beside a convulsing infant. The mother, with four small children and little English, served order and dignity alongside soup. Everything was clean. The children washed unbidden. The man had carved a home from raw timber with a hand-dug cellar and the precision of pride.

There, in that cramped room heavy with woodsmoke and worry, she remembered why she had come. Not just to practice medicine—but to be needed by it. To hold a life in her hands, not through theories or protocols, but by instinct, steadiness, and will.

Food was a battle of its own. Milk was rare. Fruit a memory. Pork and beans—ubiquitous. She came from a world of polished silver and answered bells, but now fried her own eggs and boiled her own potatoes. The lessons Clara and Henrietta had insisted on before she left England—on boiling, peeling, preserving—became scripture. Still, the gifts overwhelmed her: too many carrots, too much milk. Even generosity could be a kind of hunger.

She was invited often. One Sunday, Bill Schamehorn grinned and told her, "You'd better come over and get a fill-up of peas by 1:30." She dined with fourteen others on potatoes, raspberries, roast, and laughter. She left with a sack of peas and the smell of sun-warmed dirt in her skirt.

Crops were nearing harvest. One man, after eighteen months on his claim, watched his wheat ripen like a second chance. If it failed, so did his future. Nothing was promised here, except that the earth would demand everything.

She came to know the Métis and Indigenous communities not as subjects, but as neighbors. One man, wincing through broken English, came with a toothache. She ushered him inside. The tooth, despite warnings it would be difficult, slid free. "Looks like it wasn't as tricky as they told you," she said, and he laughed in his own language.

After he left, she stood alone in the silence of the room, the extracted tooth still in her hand. Not a patient chart in sight. No sterilized tray or white coat. And yet, for the first time in weeks, she felt entirely herself.

Word spread. A woman came from Carcajou—one hundred miles—for help.

She learned to listen to silences. Métis visitors would sit, sometimes saying nothing for minutes, the room filling not with words but presence. She waited, learned the rhythm, let trust come slow.

She learned pieces of Cree. Taystigwanan moskeke—

headache medicine. Aspirin. They called her moskeke wenou. Medicine woman.

East of her home, she visited a tight-knit Métis settlement. She tended wounds, colds, broken fingers. She was drawn to Mrs. Blue—a fierce hunter who said, "Gee-whiz! I shoot um moose, shoot um bear! I no frightened!"

Mrs. Blue brought moose meat. Brought stories. Brought laughter that punched through the solemnity of the bush. She taught Mary something no textbook had offered: how joy could sit beside hardship without apology.

Sometimes, on the trail home, she paused—the hush so deep it seemed even her breath dared not speak.

The road lay empty, her boots dusted, the sound of breathing loud in the stillness.

It was in those spaces between—between places, between people—where solitude bloomed.

Not loneliness, but that sharp, echoing kind that reminded her how far she'd come to be here.

She walked the road back home with that joy in her pockets. The wildflowers still clung to the edge of the ditch. The sun was lower now, casting long shadows of a place that had not tamed her—but had claimed her just the same.

CHAPTER 39

It was midday, the sun high in the sky, spilling heat and gold across the wildflowers perched in the window box. Mary stood at the basin, sleeves rolled, lost in the small rhythm of dishwashing—its clink and clatter a faint metronome to the silence of the north.

A knock at the door broke the hush. She dried her hands quickly and answered. On the stoop stood a young Métis woman, eyes low, body half-turned as if already preparing to leave. Mary offered a gentle smile and gestured her inside. The woman stepped over the threshold, hesitant. Silence followed, thick and taut. Mary pulled out a chair, but the woman didn't sit. After a moment, her shoulders tightened, and without a word, she turned and walked back into the bright white of day.

Mary followed, shielding her eyes against the sun. She found the woman crouched in the grass beside the porch, hands buried in the stalks as though seeking grounding from the earth itself.

"I won't hurt you," she said softly. "Can you tell me what you need?"

The woman didn't look up. Mary crouched beside her, meeting her at eye level. "What can I do?"

A long pause. Then, barely audible: "Baby."

Mary's heart shifted. "You stay here," she said, already heading inside for her bag.

They walked together, wordless, down the dusty path toward a camp three miles east. The young woman walked ahead, not quite beside her, yet not leaving her behind. Mary watched the line of her back—rigid but not unkind—and thought of the weight between them: language, history, pain. Still, she followed.

She tried a question: "Your baby? Someone else's?"

The woman gave no reply. But her eyes flicked forward, and that, too, was an answer.

They arrived in silence. Dogs barked. Children paused their play to stare. Smoke curled from fires, curling through spruce and pine. The camp pulsed with quiet activity. The woman led her to a tent, where beadwork shimmered on a flap. A woman emerged—older, eyes lined with wind and time.

"You help?" she asked.

"Yes," she said. "Where?"

Inside the tent, she hesitated at the threshold. The air was pungent with preserved meat and smoke. A deer bladder hung from the central post. Flies hummed in the heat. She caught her breath, covered her nose instinctively. A moment later, she dropped her hand. She was here to serve, not shrink.

Beneath a blanket, something stirred. She knelt and gently drew it back. A six-month-old infant lay there, cheeks too flushed, breath too shallow. She pressed her stethoscope to the tiny chest. Faint beats. Heat radiating from the skin. Meningitis, almost certainly.

"Oh dear heaven," she whispered, the words escaping before she could stop them.

She called the young woman inside. The mother entered, and the sight of the child stole the air from her lungs. She dropped beside Mary, reaching. Mary placed the baby into her arms with trembling care.

"I'm so sorry," she said. "She is too far gone. Your baby never had a chance."

The mother cradled her daughter close and began to sing—low, steady, the notes slipping between grief and reverence. Mary knelt there a moment longer, hand on the edge of the blanket, listening to a lullaby that did not need translation.

Outside, she walked slowly through the camp. The air pressed heavy on her chest. This was the other side of medicine—the part no books prepared you for. Not the saving, but the witnessing. The bearing of it.

The trail back was long and hot. Grief clung to her like the dust on her boots. Her mouth was dry, her eyes smarting, her hands numb with helplessness. The silence of the bush pressed in around her.

She walked slowly, each step a quiet reckoning. The child's flushed face lingered in her mind—not as a failure, but as a weight. She had seen death before. But out here, it felt closer. Wilder. Less sterile. A part of the land, like the rivers and the wind.

She had held the baby not as a doctor in a clinic but as a woman in a tent, breathing the smoke and sorrow of another life. No charts. No protocols. Just breath, fading. A lullaby. A mother's grief.

What was her place in all this?

She had crossed an ocean to serve—but days like this reminded her that service was not always salvation. Sometimes, it was simply presence. Witness. Kneeling in the dirt beside a woman singing her child to sleep for the last time.

She felt small beneath the northern sky. Small, and tired. But not broken.

The land did not allow for breaking. Only bending.

Near her home, she saw three Métis visitors seated on her woodpile. One of them—familiar—rose slightly at her approach. The man whose tooth she had once extracted.

"Doc," he greeted. "Hello, Doc."

His smile was warm, his presence calm. With him were two children, wide-eyed, curious. He gestured: first at his mouth, then at the boy's. "Tooth out."

The simplicity of it caught her off guard. After the weight of the day, this—this small, ordinary request—felt like grace.

"Alright," she said. "Let's take a look."

She sat on the floor, knees cracking, bag open. The children hesitated. She softened her face, recalling the old tricks—how to lower herself to their world without condescension.

"You ever meet the tooth fairy?" she asked, eyes sparkling. "She tells me all her secrets."

Their eyes lit with wary intrigue. She showed them a spoon. "Magic wand," she whispered. "But it only works if you're very brave."

The boy edged forward. His sister followed. With practiced ease, Mary coaxed him into a grin and plucked the tooth cleanly. He blinked. Then grinned wider.

He leapt to his feet, dancing in place. The others laughed. She did too, the sound bursting from her like sunlight through clouds.

Fresh and defiant, laughter filled the little room. Not in spite of grief, but beside it. As it always was, in the north.

She looked at the boy, at his gap-toothed smile, at his sister clutching her doll, at the man who had brought them—and for a moment, her sorrow receded. Not erased. But softened.

This was the work. This was the why.

She wasn't sure she could save everyone.

But maybe, just maybe, she could still help them smile.

She closed the door behind them, the sound echoing in the quiet house. Her shoulders sagged, her hands still smelling faintly of clove and tooth powder. The grief was still there—low, persistent—but it had loosened its grip.

Out here, joy and sorrow traveled together. She had learned that today.

And she would rise again tomorrow, for whoever might knock next.

CHAPTER 40

The night had closed over her cabin like a soft quilt, stitched with silence and the faint rustle of spruce boughs. Inside, the living room glowed golden with the flicker of an oil lamp, its wick whispering in time with the notes of Moonlight Sonata spinning from the gramophone. The music curled like smoke in the quiet room, tender and melancholic.

She sat curled in her chair, a British magazine open in her lap, fingers resting lightly on a page she hadn't turned in several minutes. The familiar print, the clipped advertisements for hair tonic and seaside holidays—they belonged to a life that felt impossibly distant. Outside, a wolf howled once, and silence followed. Her throat tightened. The day replayed in fragments: a child's tooth clutched in a proud hand, a baby's breath shallow and fading. Her vision blurred. She pulled the magazine to her chest, held it as if it could anchor her, and wept. For what exactly, she couldn't say. For the baby, yes. For England, perhaps. For the fragile ache of choosing a life she hadn't yet grown into.

Dawn came quietly. The light spilled like butter across the pine floorboards, gentle on her swollen eyes. A sharp knock broke the hush. She blinked, disoriented, then moved to the window. A man stood beside a horse.

By the time she flung open the door, she had her bearings.

"Your horse, as promised," Joe Bissette grinned.

Excitement crackled through her fatigue. "Give me a minute for warm clothes, and I'll be right there."

She returned moments later, coat thrown over her shoulders, boots hastily laced. Outside, two men hammered a hitching post into the frozen ground. The gelding—tall, amber-coated—stood tethered, steam curling from his nostrils. Mary paused. Her heart knocked once against her ribs, then settled into wonder.

"He's beautiful," she said.

Joe nodded, his voice practical. "Gelding. Well-tempered. Broke and comfortable. We call him Danny, but you can rename him."

She stepped closer, palm extended. Danny sniffed, snorted softly. She ran her hand along his jaw, then down his neck. "Hi, Danny."

Joe gestured to the saddle. "It'll feel like hoisting a wardrobe, but you'll build muscle. Cinch tight—he's a bloater. Watch his shoes. We'll deliver hay later today."

"Thank you," she said, meeting his eyes. "He's a gift. Truly."

When they left, she lingered. The saddle was heavy. Awkward. She managed it with effort, gritting her teeth against the awkward tilt. Once mounted, Danny shifted beneath her, but she adjusted, and found her center. The prairie opened before them, gold and green in the slanting morning light.

She talked as they rode, the way one might to an old friend—of England, of moonlight and medicine, of babies born and lost. Danny's ears flicked with each word.

Later, emboldened, she nudged him into a trot. The wind peeled past her cheeks. She laughed aloud, breathless and raw. They crested a hill, and Danny bolted downhill without warning, hooves flying. She clung on, heart hammering, more exhilarated than afraid. By the time he slowed, she was flushed and grinning.

"Easy, Danny. We're in this together," she murmured.

The landscape unfurled like scripture: brooks singing over stone, jackpines swaying in prayer. This wasn't escape; it was expansion. With each ride, her confidence grew. She learned the saddle's heft, the language of reins and pressure, the precise tuck of her medical saddlebags.

They carried tinctures, bandages, and forceps. The prairie carried her.

The trails were no more than whispers through grass and timber, curving always—to avoid muskeg, to skirt old trees. When a storm felled branches across the known path, no one cleared it. They carved new ways through. She understood: the north didn't ask permission. It required adaptation.

And she adapted.

When Danny arrived, so too did Brutus, her Great Dane pup, returned from the construction gang who had looked after him in Edmonton. He bounded from the wagon like a stormcloud with paws. Six times the food. Six times the joy. His appetite was monstrous; his affection, immediate. She named him Brutus for the contradiction—a colossus with the soul of a shadow.

With him came a new rhythm to her cabin. His paws clattered across the floorboards like hooves over ice. He steamed up windows with his breath and dragged in muddy pawprints with every bound. At night, he curled beside the stove, rising and falling with sleep like a tide—his warmth a wordless reassurance in the dark.

Her small house became a haven.

Horse. Dog. Doctor.

A trio against the vastness.

On her longest medical runs, Danny would carry her over 150 miles in a week. Brutus kept pace, galloping beside them, his tongue lolling. The three of them formed a silhouette on the horizon—a woman stitched to the land, her companions loyal and silent.

In their company, Mary found something she hadn't yet named. Not quite peace. Not quite belonging. But a kind of rootedness. A sense that, out here, even in sorrow, one could carve joy from silence.

And for the first time since stepping off the boat in Quebec, she didn't feel lost.

She felt home.

CHAPTER 41

The prairie rarely gave rest, and Mary hadn't expected any. Her patients came like weather fronts—quiet, sudden, relentless. The job demanded not just intellect, but endurance. There were few illnesses, but a flood of accidents: five fractures in as many weeks. Even four patients could overwhelm when scattered across eleven miles north and seven south.

One case, in particular, consumed her days and thoughts. A seven-year-old girl fifteen miles north had suffered a compound fracture and a dislocated elbow. It was her twelve-year-old brother, Max, who came for help.

At one o'clock in the morning, Brutus barked. She lit a lantern and opened the door to find Max—soaked with cold, eyes wide but resolute.

"My dad sent me to get you," he said.

He said he wasn't tired. He lied.

She brought him in and sat him by the stove. Brutus padded over, offering a warm tongue and silent company.

"Let me get dressed and pick up my things," she said, already moving. She loaded her medical bags, dressed in layers, and threw open the door. Brutus leapt to the threshold, already alert to the journey ahead. Moonlight silvered the shack and Danny's waiting shape.

She saddled him in one strong heave. "You're going to be fine," she murmured, adjusting the cinch.

"Lead the way," she told Max.

They trotted into the cold, star-pricked dark. She glanced at Max's thin coat, his bare hands. He insisted he was fine. The boy had the grit of a grown man, but she worried just the same.

Five miles in, they reached the first creek. His horse stumbled, then limped. She dismounted and checked the leg.

"Looks like we're walking from here."

They pressed on—Max pulling his horse, Mary following with Brutus trotting ahead.

Max spoke of bear tracks spotted days before. The woods pressed in, and even Danny seemed uneasy. The wind shifted.

Then Brutus barked—sharp, insistent, a tear through the quiet.

They froze.

Brutus darted down the trail, his dark shape swallowed by trees. The horses danced under their reins. Max's horse flinched and sidestepped.

A bear stood thirty feet off, its fur silvered by moonlight, its breath steaming in the cold. The moon caught its eyes—glass-bright, unreadable. Brutus crouched low, growling deep in his chest. Danny pawed the ground. Her fingers tightened on the reins.

"Max, hold your horse steady. Talk to him. Keep moving."

She turned to Danny. "Easy, easy," she whispered, running a hand along his neck.

Her voice rode calm over the racket in her chest. The bear hadn't moved, but she knew the wrong sound, the wrong step, could tip the balance. She kept her posture loose, her words low.

"We're okay," she said. "We'll walk past, nice and steady. No surprises."

Max echoed her. "It's alright, boy. We're okay."

Together, they edged forward. The bear remained, unmoving. Brutus stilled—tense, alert. The air felt tight as wire.

Then they were past.

She let out a slow breath. Her limbs trembled with the aftershock. She glanced at Max.

"You handled that well," she said—and knew it was true.

Brutus returned at her whistle, brushing against her leg. She scratched behind his ear, grateful beyond words.

By the time they arrived, dawn softened the sky. Purple, pink, and gold bled into the horizon. Max ran inside. She stabled Danny, checked her bags, and followed.

Inside, she treated the girl with quiet focus. The family, grateful and worn, offered her breakfast. She accepted. Brutus lay at her feet, half-dozing—alert even in rest.

Later, as she rode home beneath the rising sun, her thoughts turned to the night behind her. The creek. The bear. The boy. Brutus.

The prairie had returned to quiet. But something in her had not.

That night had drawn a new line in her understanding—between beauty and danger, between confidence and caution. She would walk her rounds differently now. Quieter. More aware of the listening trees.

And Brutus—she would trust him with her life.

In the wilderness, nothing came expected. Danger didn't announce itself. You read the wind. Listened to the trees. Trusted the silence.

Brutus had known. She would listen harder now.

Every ride brought something new. She had learned to stay ready.

Not just for broken bones and bleeding flesh.

But for the pause in the woods.

The flick of an ear.

The moonlit eyes of a watching bear.

And the boy who didn't flinch.

CHAPTER 42

Under the warm hush of a late August sun, the new bridge stood proud—ribbons tied like garlands to its railings, shimmering in the breeze. It arched over the river not just as a span of timber and bolts, but as a promise. Applause rippled as a few cars rolled slowly through the fluttering streamers, the crowd's energy buoyant with the joy of progress.

Mary stood just off the gravel approach, watching. Conversation swelled around her, laughter rising like birdsong. Dressed neatly for the occasion, she was composed but alert, her thoughts split between the dignitaries soon to arrive and the wilderness that crouched just beyond the tree line.

The Premier, John E. Brownlee, was expected, along with several local officials. But it was the sight of Frank Jackson—arm raised, smile bright—that caught her more off guard. He was waving from a distance, striding toward her with that easy confidence she remembered.

"Hello, Mary," he said, his voice low and warm.

She returned the smile, guarded but genuine. "Well, hello, Mr. Jackson. It's been a while."

They began walking toward the picnic area, the hum of the crowd trailing behind them. He launched into tales of work—roads built, supplies hauled, contracts negotiated. She listened, her gaze occasionally drifting to the shifting edges of the trees.

"You do sound busy," she said, half-teasing, half-serious. "So, you came a hundred miles just for a bridge opening?"

"Well, it is important to me. The road'll reach my camp soon. This opens up trade."

"Ah. A capitalist, then."

He grinned. "I won't say no to a good opportunity."

They settled on a quilt laid under a trembling aspen, its pale leaves flickering like coins in the wind. She passed him a sandwich wrapped in wax paper. Around them, children dashed between baskets and barrels. Someone strummed a guitar off-key.

Premier Brownlee took to the makeshift stage. His voice rang out, formal and resonant. She applauded politely with the others, her mind half on his words, half elsewhere.

"And we must recognize Dr. Mary Percy," Brownlee announced, voice swelling with performative pride. "For her unwavering commitment to this region, where the nearest doctor is more than a hundred miles away—her work has been nothing short of indispensable."

A spotlight of applause. Faces turned. She flushed, stood slowly as he offered his hand to help her up. His palm was rough, steady.

"Look who's aiding the capitalists now," he whispered.

She narrowed her eyes and bit back a smile, returning to her seat as the crowd quieted. Her attention, as ever, drifted to the woods—to the slight shifts in shadow, the whispers between leaves.

Frank noticed. "Something bothering you?"

She hesitated. Then: "There've been bear sightings lately. Close ones. Brutus had a standoff just last week."

His brow furrowed. "A bear this close?"

She nodded, her eyes still scanning the tree line. "With more settlers, more food around, they're curious. Hungry. I worry about the kids, especially."

He was quiet for a moment. "You keeping a rifle near?"

She looked at him, the question landing heavy. "I've never needed one. Not in Birmingham. Not even here. Until now."

"Out here, it's not about using it. It's about having it. Even a warning shot changes a bear's mind."

The words settled in. A part of her resisted—guns still belonged to another world, another version of herself. But the wilderness didn't care about versions.

Children shrieked with joy nearby. Her gaze followed them, then returned to him.

"Alright. But you'll have to show me. Nothing fancy. Just enough to keep us safe."

He leaned back on his elbows, grinning. "Dinner and rifle lessons. That's a trade I'll take."

"We'll shoot at cans," she said. "And maybe I'll shoot

better than you."

He laughed, the sound easy, rolling. "Only if you're lucky."

They lingered on the blanket, passing food, letting the hum of the celebration fold around them. The bridge stood tall behind them, ribbons still fluttering, the wind carrying their laughter into the trees.

And though Mary watched the woods, alert to movement and rustle, she felt—for the first time in weeks—less alone in the watching.

CHAPTER 43

The sun hung low in the sky, casting a warm, golden glow over Mary's homestead. The wilderness buzzed with life—the rustle of grass, the hum of insects, the distant call of a loon. She stood beside Frank in the clearing, rifle in her hands, its cool metal pressing into her palms like a truth she hadn't wanted to hold. This was more than a lesson in marksmanship. It was a reckoning.

"First rule—always treat it as loaded," he said, his voice both firm and gentle.

She nodded, adjusting her stance. Her movements were awkward at first, but she mimicked his posture, grounding herself, finding balance. The rifle felt alien—like wearing someone else's courage.

"It's about being calm," he reminded her. "Bears can smell fear. They can see weakness. But they'll turn from strength. Sometimes just noise will do."

The lesson unfolded slowly. She fired at rusted cans balanced on a log, each shot echoing like a decision.

Her aim improved. Her grip steadied.

"You're getting it," he said, smiling.

She lowered the rifle, breathless. "It's empowering. To know I can handle this."

He nodded. "It's not about wanting to shoot. It's knowing you can, if it comes to it."

As the sun dipped further, they moved inside to cook. The kitchen glowed softly with lamplight. She fumbled with ingredients, laughing at her own inexperience. He listened to her stories of Birmingham—the brick hospital walls, the polished floors, the hush of children's wards. He didn't interrupt. Just watched, absorbed.

Dinner was half-burnt potatoes and over-salted stew, but neither of them minded. They sat close, shoulders brushing, laughter easy, silences warm.

Then came the knock.

A young boy on horseback. Solemn-eyed. "Dr. Percy, Mrs. Elkins is ill."

She was already rising. "I'll come right away."

"I'll go with you," Frank said, already gathering his things.

The twilight was bleeding into indigo as they saddled up. Brutus loped beside them, ears alert, tongue lolling. The forest sighed around them. Her heart beat steady. She had done this before. She would do it again.

Then Brutus barked. Not a casual alert. A warning. Fierce. Urgent.

Frank raised a hand. They stopped.

He dismounted. "Something's wrong. Stay here."

"Frank?"

He grabbed his flashlight and rifle. "Call Brutus. Hold the horses."

She obeyed, her hands tightening on the reins. The trees loomed. The wind stilled. Brutus's barking spun through the dark like thread through a needle.

He vanished into the trees.

Her breath caught. Then came the rumble—like stones sliding down a ravine. The horses jerked, eyes rolling. Danny reared. Her grip slipped. She hit the ground hard, the air punched from her lungs.

Pain flared, but she scrambled to her knees.

A shape exploded from the woods—a black bear, massive and thundering.

Frank shouted. His rifle clattered away. The bear lunged, striking him hard. He crumpled to the earth.

"Frank!"

Brutus chased after the bear, snarling, driving it back. But it wasn't retreating. It turned again. Toward her.

She stood. Blood in her mouth. Adrenaline in her bones.

Remember, it's not just about shooting. Bears turn from strength.

She raised her arms.

And screamed.

A raw, primal cry that tore through the woods. The bear halted, grunting. Its eyes locked on hers. Intelligent. Hungry.

She shook. She didn't want to hurt it. It was a creature, not a monster. But it was too close. Too wild.

She spotted Frank's rifle. Ten feet away. Her feet moved before she could think. She dove, rolled, caught it.

Be loud. Scare it away.

She cocked the rifle and fired into the air.

The crack split the sky.

The bear flinched. But didn't flee.

And in that suspended moment—heart pounding, ears ringing—she locked eyes with it. The creature didn't rage. It existed—wild, immense, alive. Her breath caught. She didn't want this. Not the blood. Not the end of something so magnificent.

Please go, she thought. Just go.

But the bear held its ground. Its massive shoulders rolled forward, a grunt rumbling from its chest. It had made its choice.

And she—still trembling, still hoping—knew what hers had to be.

Brutus barked again. The bear charged.

She lowered her aim.

She fired.

The sound was thunder.

The bear collapsed.

Silence.

Brutus approached, slow, ears back.

She stared at the bear. Its breath, gone. Its vastness, stilled. The silence roared. She had done this. Her hands. Her will. There would be no going back.

She dropped the rifle. Her hands shook violently. She ran to Frank, who was stirring, bruised, dazed.

"Frank! Are you hurt?"

He coughed. "No broken bones. Wind's knocked out of

me."

She knelt beside him and then—suddenly, without warning—she wept. Great, racking sobs that spilled from her like floodwater.

He reached for her. "Hey. Hey, it's over. We're okay."

But she wasn't crying only for relief.

She cried because she had killed something. Because he might've died. Because Brutus might've died. Because she had believed, deep down, that this land was noble, quiet, healing—and now it had shown her its teeth.

"I didn't want to do it," she choked out.

"I know."

She looked at the bear's body. Beautiful even in death. A part of the land that would no longer move through it.

He cupped her face gently. She didn't flinch. "You did what you had to. You saved our lives. You saved mine."

Brutus circled them, still watchful.

Trying to ease the weight, he said quietly, "Well… looks like our tin can practice paid off." His voice was careful, almost tender. "Though you didn't have to show off that much on your first try."

She let out a broken laugh, the sound catching in her

throat. A silence followed—just long enough for the trees to settle again, for the forest to remember its quiet.

"I'll never eat bear meat," she said finally, wiping her eyes with the back of her hand. "That's all yours."

He managed a smile. "Oh come on. You haven't even tried it with rosemary."

She groaned, but it was softer now.

"You, Dr. Percy," he said, rising with a wince, "are officially a wilderness warrior."

"A wilderness warrior with a strong aversion to culinary experiments."

He looked at her, serious again. "Still. You were brave. Really brave."

She turned her gaze back to the bear. Its body was still. Monumental. "I was terrified," she whispered. "But I did it anyway." Then, more quietly: "I hope that still counts."

A breeze moved through the trees. The scent of pine and iron lingered. She looked at the bear again. Death had a shape now. And it would follow her into every quiet walk, every moonlit ride. Not fear—but memory.

He held her close and whispered, "It does."

"Think I'll stick to being a doctor," she said. "But...

thank you. For everything."

They stood in silence. The kind that follows survival.

Then he touched her shoulder. "Ready for the next adventure?"

She nodded, voice low. "As long as it doesn't involve bear meat or flying hooves."

Brutus led, ears alert, tail low, searching for the horses.

They followed—two shadows stitched by moonlight—back into the waiting dark.

CHAPTER 44

In the heart of the Battle River Prairie, late August arrived on a hush of frost. The air, sharp and clear, shimmered against the golden spill of dawn. Mary stoked the stove, the scent of wood smoke curling through her modest cabin, chasing out the chill. The eggs sizzled. Bacon spat. Her breath fogged the windowpane as she looked out—sunlight glinting off dew-soaked grass, the world painted in quiet promise.

Then came the knock.

Urgent. Disruptive. A voice followed, hoarse and winded. "Doc? Doc? Are you there?"

She wiped her hands, heart already quickening.

A telegraph worker stood at her door, face pale and drawn, his clothes dust-streaked. "One of the fellas fell off the top of the pole. It's bad, Doc. Real bad. We need you."

She was moving before he finished speaking. "One moment," she said, already in her consulting room, medical bag in hand. Her eyes caught the cooling skillet on the stove. She exhaled once, deeply. Another breakfast lost to duty.

The air outside tasted of early autumn—bittersweet, metallic. She mounted quickly, following the man across trails hemmed with dying grass and crooked trees. The land, so alive with color, felt momentarily suspended, watching.

At the site, she dismounted hard. Blood darkened the earth beneath a slumped body. The man's arm bent where it should not. His nose streamed red.

Mary dropped beside him.

"Did anyone move him?"

"No, Doc. He's where he fell. Is he—?"

"Quiet now. Let me see."

Her tone cut clean through their panic. They backed away. She leaned in.

"Sir, can you hear me? I'm Dr. Percy. You've had a fall, but we're going to help you."

He stirred faintly. The whisper of life.

Her hands moved with precision. Spine first. Always the spine. Her fingers, practiced and sure, felt for fractures while her mind counted symptoms like prayer beads. Paralysis. Blood loss. Shock.

Empathy bloomed and surged—briefly. Then she tucked it aside. There would be time for softness later.

A voice called behind her. "They're sending Wop May. Plane'll land in the open field."

She nodded without looking. "Good."

"What's his name?"

"Bill, Doc."

"Bill," she murmured, anchoring him to something human.

She watched his fingers. A twitch—barely—but it was there.

"You," she said, pointing to the nearest man. "Support his head. Firmly. Don't move unless I say."

"Got it."

She reached for splints, wrapped his broken arm. "Brace yourself. This'll hurt."

A hiss of pain. But no scream.

Then, louder, to the group: "We need boards. Straight, flat. We're building a stretcher. His spine may be compromised. We move him wrong, he won't walk again."

Their movements scattered like startled birds, then aligned.

One man returned. "The field's a half mile back."

"Then we'll meet him there," she said. Her voice held.

When the stretcher was ready, she hovered like a hawk. "On my count. One, two, three."

They lifted. Slow. Controlled.

She walked beside them through the trail, hands near, voice steady.

Her mind flicked to a boy in Birmingham. A crushed pelvis. Too late. That had been a hospital with tile floors and orderlies and machines. Here, it was moss and splinters and silence.

The field opened ahead, sunlit and swaying. The plane's low hum grew louder, like a promise threading through sky.

She kept her gaze on Bill. Still breathing. Still with her.

Dust billowed as the plane touched down. Wop May stepped out—tall, composed, his eyes scanning quickly.

"Dr. Percy?"

"Thank you for coming."

"Call me Wop. Let's not waste time."

"Spinal injury suspected. We've stabilized him."

He nodded. "Let's get him in."

They lifted again. In sync now, their hands sure. The wilderness, for once, held its breath.

The cabin was tight but prepared. She settled beside Bill, checking straps, watching his pulse.

Wop turned. "You flying with us?"

"I am."

"Then let's go."

She looked out the door once—at the men, at the field, at the trembling grass—and then the plane rose.

The sky closed beneath them. The wilderness fell away.

She watched Bill. Listened to the engine's steady roar. Her hands rested on her bag. Her thoughts on landing.

Even here, in the wild edge of Alberta, medicine was not a calling—it was a covenant. Today, she had answered.

And tomorrow, she would again.

CHAPTER 45

High above the Battle River Prairie, she sat in the narrow hum of Wop May's aircraft, the smell of oil and canvas mingling with the cool draft that whispered through the seams. Beside her, Bill lay strapped and still, his breaths shallow but steady. Her eyes stayed on him until they didn't—until the plane tilted gently, revealing the world below, and something in her chest unlatched.

It struck her then: this was her first time in the sky.

The thought brought a sudden, irrational panic—a surge of vertigo and wonder, of being untethered from the earth she had so painstakingly claimed as her own. Her hand found the metal brace near the window, clinging out of instinct more than fear. She leaned forward, cautiously, peering out.

The land stretched—vast, unknowable, beautiful. What she had ridden over for months now unfurled beneath her like a living map, stitched with rivers and ridgelines, patches of pine, and the ghost-thin tracings of trails. It wasn't just terrain. It was memory.

But it was disorienting, too. A world turned sideways. The angle, the distance, the sheer scope of it—she struggled for a moment to place herself. The cabin? The river? Even the sun felt somehow unfamiliar from up here.

Then—there. The glint of water. The silver snake of the Battle River carving through forest. She followed it with her eyes, heart climbing in her throat.

A bridge came into view, its planks a faint scratch in the green. Then the road. Winding like thread between birch stands and pastures. And finally—her cabin. A smudge beneath the trees. Unmistakable.

Her whole face lit. A small laugh caught in her throat.

There.

Mary traced the road from her place to the one-room schoolhouse, then further to the Bissette's store and farm. Even from the air, she could imagine Sally feeding the chickens, and Joe mending a fence. The realization was profound: this wasn't just wilderness anymore—it was hers. She could map it with her heart.

That humble, weather-beaten shelter. Where she had arrived uncertain and green. Where she had bled and stitched and laughed and ached. It had once felt like exile. Now it glowed like belonging.

She glanced to Wop, his hands steady on the controls, then back to the window.

They passed above scattered homesteads—cleared patches with laundry lines, smoke curling from chimneys, horses standing in sun-baked fields. Dots of human hope, stubborn and small. She imagined the lives inside. Their grit. Their loneliness. Their unspoken alliances with wind and cold and time. These were her neighbors now, not by proximity, but by pact.

Wop's voice cut through the drone. "We'll be in Peace River in twenty."

"He's stable," she said softly, brushing a loose hair from Bill's forehead. "But I'll watch him."

He smiled, then gestured toward the view. "Still. Worth a look."

She turned again to the window, to the endless cathedral of sky and wilderness. And there, in the hush between engine growl and wind, she let herself feel it—the quiet revelation.

She had once dreamed of India. Of far-flung places with bright colors and strange sounds. But life, in its secret wisdom, had brought her here instead—to a place where color lived in sky and moss, where silence was rich with meaning, where hardship revealed the marrow of who you were.

This was her India. This wild, relentless, beautiful place.

And she, somehow, belonged.

As the plane banked gently toward the river valley, she rested her palm on Bill's chest to feel its rise. The hum of the engine vibrated through her bones. She closed her eyes for a moment—not to sleep, but to remember this exact feeling. Not fear. Not fatigue. But something else.

Altitude. Perspective. Flight.

They landed rough. A bump, a tilt, a quick breath held between worlds. Then the wheels found earth and the engine groaned into stillness.

Wop opened the door and swung out onto the dirt, boots crunching. "Welcome to Peace River," he said with a grin. "Bit smoother than a bobsled, anyway."

Climbing down stiffly from the flight, her hands still trembled faintly from adrenaline and altitude. The sun was lower now, casting long shadows across the field.

Wop May and the ground crew worked in sync, every gesture measured for safety. Together, they lifted Bill from the aircraft and transferred him to the waiting ambulance, every gesture measured for safety.

Mary turned one last time to the sky, to the wide blue

that had shown her the shape of her life from above. Then to the ground beneath her boots—this strange country that no longer felt foreign.

"Not bad for your first flight," Wop said, handing her the medical bag. "You didn't scream once."

She gave him a sidelong glance. "I was too busy memorizing the view."

He tipped his cap, voice quiet now. "That's how you know you belong. When the sky starts feeling like part of the map."

Mary didn't reply. Just smiled.

CHAPTER 46

With Bill safely aboard the ambulance, Mary climbed in beside him, her gloved hand resting lightly on his shoulder as they bumped toward Irene Cottage Hospital. She had done all she could in the air. Now, she released the reins. For the first time that day, her breath came slow.

Stepping out of the ambulance, she squared her shoulders, fatigue tucked behind purpose. Inside, the hospital pulsed with quiet precision—orderlies brisk, nurses murmuring in clipped tones. It struck her as strange and familiar all at once. Clean linoleum. Bright lights. A world apart from her mossy trails and horsehide saddle.

They wheeled him through the emergency ward, and she walked alongside, briefing the attending physician as they moved. Her voice was steady, each word a tile in the bridge from field to facility.

Dr. Patel met her at the doors of the exam room. "He

took quite a fall," he said, already assessing.

"Yes. I'm concerned about the spine. We braced him best we could."

Dr. Patel nodded. "Let's get him in for imaging. We'll take it from here."

She gave a final nod, brushing Bill's hair back once before stepping aside. As he disappeared into the sterile brightness, a quiet loosened inside her. The fear, the adrenaline—it receded like a tide. She had carried him far enough. Now others would carry him further.

A nurse approached with a clipboard. "Doctor Percy? Could you note his condition during transport?"

Mary accepted it, her pen moving in practiced rhythm. When she handed it back, the nurse glanced up and offered a small smile. "You brought him in alive. That counts for a lot."

Out in the night again, her legs ached with the memory of the ride, the flight, the strain of worry. Peace River's main street glowed soft under gaslights. Ten o'clock rang from the town clock, solemn and clear.

The sky unfurled in a curtain of green silk. The northern lights rippled above, vast and slow. She stood beneath them, hands in her pockets, breath visible. The spectacle asked nothing of her. It simply was.

Thoughts of Frank. Of their stolen moments and quiet talk. Of Danny and Brutus waiting back home. She felt the ache of it—not longing, not loneliness, but something warmer. A recognition.

The Peace River Hotel was lit like a hearth when she reached it. Inside, laughter and piano chords spilled from the lounge. The front desk sat empty.

She pushed the lounge door open and stepped into the hum. A few heads turned. Trail-worn, coat dusty, boots crusted with prairie, she did not fit the wallpapered quiet of the place. Still, she held herself steady.

"Excuse me," she said, glancing around. "Is anyone available at the front desk?"

A voice rose from a table near the fire. "Dr. Percy?"

Madeline.

Her face lit with recognition and joy. Mary's weariness softened.

They moved to a quieter corner. The chatter receded. The familiarity of another woman from the trail—a kindred soul—unwound something tight in her chest.

"I remember Jarvie," Madeline said warmly. "And Clyde. You always volunteered for the worst shifts."

Mary smiled faintly. "Still do, some days."
Introductions followed—Sylvie, Charlotte, Doctors Henderson and Markham. Names she repeated with a smile, though she knew they'd blur by morning. Still, there was grace in being welcomed, even briefly.

They poured her tea and leaned in close as she spoke—about the telegraph boy, about Brutus and Danny, about the bridge finally finished, about the smell of spruce in spring and the sound of ravens circling overhead. Her words painted the prairie in long strokes—wild, harsh, beautiful. And at first, they listened.

But something shifted. Just slightly. A pause too long before a polite laugh. A raised brow. The glance someone gave her boots, still flecked with mud. The way Sylvie's eyes lingered on the worn seams of her sleeves.

"So you ride out alone?" asked Charlotte, incredulous.

"Of course she does," said one of the doctors, amused. "Just look what she's wearing. I'd last five minutes out there."

Laughter—sharp, well-meaning, but edged. A kind of

admiration that cost them nothing.

Mary smiled. Or something like it.

She felt suddenly apart from them. Their coats were wool and pressed. Their hands bore no scars. They carried medicine in leather cases and returned to hotels with hot water and linen sheets. She had slept in barns. Delivered babies by lantern light. Dug bullets from flesh with no time for sterilization beyond fire and whiskey.

She wasn't ashamed. But she was seen, and not quite understood.

Madeline touched her hand gently beneath the table, her eyes different from the others—less amused, more knowing.

"I think I'll turn in," Mary said quietly, standing before the heat could rise to her cheeks.

Madeline stood, concerned. "Mary—wait. I'm sorry. They didn't mean—"

"I know," Mary said. Her voice was calm. Not cold, just final. "I just needed air."

She stepped into the night, where silence didn't judge.

Outside, the aurora still danced. And in its movement,

Mary felt steadied.

She had once doubted. Wondered if she belonged among these trees and silences. Wondered if medicine done on horseback counted the same. Even here, among doctors in pressed coats and crisp lights, she still felt like the one passing a patient into a system that wasn't quite hers.

Now she knew.
Her home waited—a cabin tucked beneath pines. Danny's warm flank. Brutus's quiet watch. And Frank, with his few words and steady gaze.

She had not merely endured. She had arrived.

In the wildness, she had not lost herself. She had become.

And the sky above—green and wide—seemed to agree.

Amidst these reflections, her thoughts drifted to Frank. She recalled the way he'd offered his support without hesitation—the shared glances, the quiet understanding, the way his presence calmed the edges of her. There was no performance in him, no pretense. Just steadiness. Just truth.

She hadn't gone looking for it. Not here, not now. And yet, it had come—unexpected as a thaw in March. A warmth, yes. But more than that: a sense of being seen. Known. Paired not in need, but in respect.

For a long while, she had thought her work would be enough. That it had to be. But standing beneath the northern lights, her boots rooted in this strange and beautiful country, she allowed herself the truth.

She loved him.

The thought rose without fanfare. Without fear. As natural as breath.
It wasn't a desperate thing, or a girlish flutter. It was a quiet knowing. A choice, already made somewhere deep in her marrow. The kind of love shaped by cold mornings, shared silences, and the grace of not having to explain yourself.

As the aurora shimmered and shifted above her, she felt it settle inside her—not a question, but a certainty. Her life had taken root here. And love, wild and luminous, had grown with it.

CHAPTER 47

In the dimly lit interior of her modest home, the evening whispered through the open windows, carrying the scent of pine and earth. She stood in her bedroom, gaze fixed on the wardrobe that housed memories of a past life. Candlelight flickered, casting dancing shadows over elegant gowns—relics from Birmingham, from ballrooms and genteel conversations, from a woman she no longer was.

She lifted one gently, letting the silk spill through her fingers. Holding it up to the mirror, she saw herself split: the woman in the gown, refined and delicate, and the woman reflected back—wind-worn, practical, steady. A physician forged in snow and saddle.

Her breath came deep. Slow. She gathered several gowns in her arms and carried them to the kitchen table. They lay there like a final offering, shimmering and silent. She sat beside them, her fingers tracing embroidery, remembering light glinting off chandeliers, the muffled hush of music through layered voices. She smiled. Not wistfully, but with a quiet acknowledgment. It had been beautiful. But it was no longer hers.

One dress, the blue one with pearl buttons at the collar, paused her hand. A memory stirred—her father, proud and teary-eyed, clasping her shoulders after her medical school graduation. "You look perfect, Mary. Just like your mother." She had glowed in that moment, unsure whether it was the gown or the gravity of what she'd become. Now, the memory felt like something she'd read once in a book, pages worn soft with time.

The scissors gleamed in the candlelight. For a moment they hovered—an instrument of both memory and metamorphosis. Then she pressed the blades to the silk. The first cut was clean. Final.

Soundless tears surprised her, not of grief but of gravity. She wasn't destroying; she was releasing. With each slice, the past shed itself, slivered into something new. Satin into strips. Lace into bandages. Elegance into utility. Her gowns were not vanishing; they were becoming something more essential.

The rhythm of her work became meditative. She thought of the lives those bandages might touch. The warmth those scraps might carry tucked in the pouch of a child's medicine kit. Her past would not be discarded—it would be sewn into the present, into the pulse of this land.

She paused at the table, scissors set down. Her gaze drifted to the window, where night deepened and the forest breathed. This land had asked everything of her—and given more in return. It had shaped her hands and spine and heart. She no longer carried the weight of needing to belong.

She did.

Her thoughts turned to Frank. Steady, silent Frank. He had entered her life like the thaw—soft and inevitable. In his presence, she had felt safe without needing to be small. His silences weren't emptiness, but space in which her thoughts could stretch and settle.

The love that grew between them had no ceremony. It had no need for gowns. It had risen in the quiet between words, in the shared work of surviving, in the brush of his hand against hers at the woodpile. It wasn't fireworks.

It was roots.

The realization came not as a revelation, but as recognition: she loved him. Fiercely. Quietly. Completely. A love formed in snowlight and sweat, in the hush of rivers and the howling dark. It didn't ask to be spoken. It simply was.

Around her, the transformed gowns glowed in the low light. Not remnants, but markers of a choice fully made.
Outside, the stars stretched over the wilderness. She held her coffee close, its warmth grounding her in the here and now.

This life. This man. This land.

Not what she had imagined.

Better.

CHAPTER 48

It was late September, and the world outside her home was softly illuminated by the first rays of dawn, casting a gentle glow over the landscape. Mary awoke to the brisk, invigorating air inside her small dwelling, her senses coming alive to the day's fresh beginnings. Brutus, her regal Great Dane with a lineage as noble as his stature, nudged her awake with his cold nose, his whines gentle yet insistent.

As she rose from the cocoon of warmth her bed provided, the chilled air caressed her skin—a stark contrast to the snug comfort of her blankets. Her feet touched the cold floor, sending a shiver up her spine. The wood stove, her steadfast ally against the harsh northern nights, glowed dimly with the remnants of last night's fire.

Approaching the stove, she added more logs, coaxing the embers back to life. The crackling sound of firewood catching flame filled the room with warmth. Outside, the world was still asleep, wrapped in the hush of dawn.

Brutus, with his thick coat and boundless energy, followed her closely, his tail wagging enthusiastically. She smiled at his antics, her heart warmed by his loyal companionship.

She filled a bucket with water and placed the kettle on the stove. The promise of a hot cup of coffee brightened the morning. Preparing breakfast was a comforting ritual, grounding her to the rhythm of life here.

Turning her attention to him, she prepared his meal. "One day, I'll teach you to tend the stove," she joked. Brutus tilted his head, perplexed and earnest.

Her gaze drifted to the window, and her breath caught. Overnight, the landscape had transformed into a winter wonderland. A thick blanket of snow covered everything, untouched and glistening.

"Oh my, look, boy, there's snow!" she exclaimed. Brutus barked in reply, bounding to the door.

A quick glance through another window revealed Danny standing beside a tree, his mane frosted. The shed door had blown open.

With urgency, she dressed and stepped outside, Brutus dashing ahead through the soft snow. The air was crisp and biting, each breath a burst of clarity.

She gently brushed snow off Danny's back and

covered him with a blanket. Guiding him back into the paddock shed, she secured the door.

With Danny settled, she paused, taking in the breathtaking stillness. The distant river was muffled beneath the snow's hush. Not a flake stirred. The world seemed to hold its breath.

Brutus bounded through the snow, barking joyfully. She packed a snowball and lobbed it at him. He leapt, missing it, then turned to chase another. Her laughter echoed in the frozen air.

The trees stood tall, their branches heavy with white. Her modest home, half-buried in snow, looked like something from a fairy tale.

She took another snowball in hand and threw it. Brutus tore off—but then stopped. Ears perked, head tilted.

Before she could call him back, he bolted.

"Brutus!" she shouted, her voice sharp. "Heel!"

But he didn't stop. He ran to the treeline.

Then she saw it: the sled. A team of dogs cutting smoothly across the powder, and at the helm, bundled in heavy winter gear—Frank.

She laughed under her breath, heart light. "Of course."

Frank slowed the sled. Brutus ran circles around him, tail wagging furiously.

"Frank, what's the occasion?" she called, warmth blooming in her chest.

"Thought I'd drop by with my sled and dogs," he said, grinning. "Time you got your own team, now that Danny'll be boarded soon."

She smiled, considering the idea with a nod.

But her eyes caught something—his hand. Bandaged.

"Frank, what happened to your hand?"

He shrugged it off. "Trap snapped. It's nothing."

"Let me look at it," she said firmly, already turning toward the house. "Come inside."

Inside, the room still held the morning chill. She moved to stoke the stove, but he was already beside it.

"Frank, you don't need to—"

"I just sledded a hundred miles to see you," he said gently. "I can manage a fire."

She watched him, her protest half-formed. He moved like he belonged there—boots brushing snow off at the door, hands steady with the kindling.

She turned away to hide the flush warming her cheeks. She brushed her hair back, adjusted her sweater. It was silly, she thought, to care how she looked. But she did.

He filled the space with ease, the scrape of logs and

soft creak of his boots grounding her. She busied herself with the kettle, but her eyes kept drifting. The set of his jaw. The curl of steam rising between them.

She gestured to the table. "Sit. Let me see that hand."

He obeyed, and she took his hand gently, unwrapping the bandage. The wound was deep but clean.

"What happened?" she asked.

"Trap line," he said. "Old one snapped on me."

She nodded, working in silence. The moment between them thickened—comfortable, charged. Her fingers grazed his skin as she cleaned the cut.

"We've never really talked," she said softly. "Not deeply."

His gaze met hers. "No. But I'd like to."

She nodded. "I know it's not easy, raising a child alone."

"Three," he said quietly. "Arthur, Louis, and little Frank."

Her hand paused. "Three boys?"

His voice was soft, tinged with memory. "Louise died after our third. Wop May helped us get her to Peace River, but it was too late."

"I wish I'd been here," she said. "Maybe I could've helped."

He shook his head. "Things happen, for good or bad. We live with them."

"Where are your sons now?"

"In Edmonton. With my parents. I'll see them after school ends."

She smiled gently. "I'd like to meet them."

"I'd like that too."

As she stitched and wrapped his hand, their nearness pulsed like a quiet heartbeat. She felt her own nerves stir—this was the first time she'd seen him since fully realizing what he meant to her. Each glance felt brighter. Each word, more weighty.

He watched her hands. "You've gotten good at this."

She smiled. "Practice. Too much of it."

When she finished, she leaned back. "You should stay the night. Rest. Supper's on me."

He looked at her, something unspoken flickering behind his eyes. "I'd like that. Can I help?"

"Your job tonight is to convalesce," she teased. "You've got Brutus and me for company. I'll try to cook something that won't poison us."

He chuckled, deep and warm. "Anything's better than my cooking. Being alone gets old."

As dusk fell, the room softened. Madame Butterfly

played from her gramophone, haunting and sweet. They moved around each other gently, like a tide turning in a quiet bay.

She set plates down, caught his eye. He was watching her.

"Something wrong?" she asked, heart quickening.

He shook his head slowly. "No. Just... nice, being here."

She looked away, smiled. Her heart thudded steady and bright.

As they ate, silence drifted in and out of their conversation like smoke. She found herself noting the line of his cheek, the way he held his fork. How easily he belonged in this room.

And when he reached across the table to pour her tea, their fingers brushed. Neither pulled away.

Later, when the fire burned low and the night held its breath around them, she stepped outside with Brutus. The snow glowed blue in the moonlight.

She looked back at the house, its window lit gold. He was still inside.

And for the first time, she knew: she wasn't alone anymore. Not in any way that mattered.

Not in her work. Not in her heart.

Not in this life she had chosen.

He was here.

And so was she.

CHAPTER 49

In the middle of December, she found herself wrapped in the hush of the Battle River Prairie, where winter reigned with quiet authority. Snow fell in elegant drifts, sculpted by the wind into crests and hollows, some rising taller than the fence posts. The land, beneath its white cloak, exhaled silence. Everything had slowed to the pace of breath.

Danny had been boarded with a farmer for the season, tucked in warm and fed on oats and rest. In his place came the dogsled—Frank's idea, a gift of both function and freedom. She'd been uncertain at first. But like medicine and migration, she had learned to adapt.

Now, dog sled and toboggan had become her carriage across the snowbound distances, the panting rhythm of the dogs her daily soundtrack. The sled's runners hissed softly over packed snow, and her hands, leather-gloved and sure, gripped the wooden rails with ease earned from trial. Their names had become music in the morning air: Scout, Pippa, Red. Brutus loped alongside like a sentinel.

A few days before Christmas, the air held a crystalline brightness, brittle and clear. Most of her rounds were done early, the morning's cases no more serious than chilblains and a cough that would pass with tea and rest. The day opened before her like a fresh page.

She turned toward the river.

A patient—old Mr. Abernathy with a heart like a clock one tick too slow—had cleared a patch of ice behind his homestead. "For skating," he'd said, as if gifting her a piece of childhood. She remembered the manicured rinks of Birmingham, girls in ribbons gliding past. Polite, practiced, predictable. This was different. This was her. She hadn't skated in years. But that morning, with her skates slung over one shoulder and a broomstick for balance, she made her way there with a determined grin.

Brutus trotted at her side, ears perked, his breath misting in bursts. The sled dogs ran ahead, yelping with delight at the crisp air, their paws kicking up little whirlwinds of powder.

The ice shone like glass under a pale sun. Trees bowed in reverence on either side, their branches heavy with snow.

She laced her skates and stepped onto the ice.

The first glide was clumsy, then another, and soon her legs remembered. She wobbled, then caught herself with a laugh, the broomstick wobbling like a clumsy dance partner. Brutus barked, concerned, as she spun slowly, arms out, scarf trailing behind her. Her laughter rang out, a clear note across the frozen hush.

She fell once. Maybe twice. Rose each time with snow on her palms and joy in her ribs. Her body knew how to fall, to shift weight, to find balance—on ice, on horseback, in the chaos of a hemorrhage.

When she tired, she collapsed in a patch of snow, limbs splayed, looking skyward as breath clouded above her. The dogs surrounded her, tongues lolling, eyes bright. She felt their heat against her sides, the press of life against the stillness.

Back at the house, she swapped skates for boots and rigged the sled. The dogs, still wild with energy, yipped and jostled as she fitted their harnesses. Brutus sat to one side, noble and unmoved, but his eyes gleamed.

She gripped the sled rails and gave a soft call. The dogs lunged forward.

They flew.

The world blurred into motion—trees flickering past, snow erupting from the sled's path, her breath lost to the rush of cold and speed. Her braid whipped behind her. Her cheeks stung with the wind.

And still she laughed.

Fields opened before her, rivers inlaid with glass. Hills crested and fell, the world dipping and rising beneath her as the sled carved its path through the wilderness. She was nowhere and everywhere. A streak of color against the white.

At that moment, she was not a doctor or daughter or woman of Birmingham. She was pulse and breath. Bone and joy.

The land gave back what she gave it: effort for beauty, solitude for clarity.

No calls came. No crises waited. Only this: wind on her face, dogs at her command, and a sky so wide it made her ache.

When she finally returned home, breathless and flushed, she lingered at the door. The sled dogs panted in the snow. Brutus circled once and lay down, content.

She turned, looked out over the trail they had carved, then up at the gathering dusk.

Snow began to fall again, soft as sleep. She had once feared the cold would undo her. Now she wore it like a second skin.

Tomorrow, she would ride.

But tonight, she would remember what it felt like to fly.

CHAPTER 50

Inside her small house, the scent of spruce mingled with the faint sweetness of scorched sugar and spice—remnants of her morning attempt at ginger cookies. The recipe, a gift from Sally Bissette tucked into a Christmas hamper, had promised holiday cheer. The result had been... less successful. The cookies sat on a chipped plate by the stove, dark around the edges, cracked like river ice. Brutus had licked one, sneezed, and walked away. Still, the effort lingered in the air, part cloves and burnt sugar.

Outside, the cold clung like a second skin, the wind rattling in gusts, persistent as memory. But within, warmth held its own.

Mary curled into her armchair beside the stove, Brutus sprawled at her feet, his chest rising and falling in a slow rhythm that matched the hush of the room. Letters lay open in her lap—thin paper from across the ocean, inked in familiar hands. She traced the words as though they were threads, drawing her backward: to candlelight in Birmingham, to holly on the mantle, to her father's laughter echoing off polished floors. She remembered Christmas mornings where silver trays gleamed and stockings bulged with trifles. The clink of glasses. The smell of beeswax and oranges. Her father, once, catching her at the top of the stairs in her dressing gown, had winked and said, "Don't let the cook see you steal the mince pies."

The comfort of recollection stung too sharply. Her world now was cedar smoke and snow, not coal dust and city bells.

She folded the letters with care. With each page returned to its envelope, she tucked away a little more of her ache. The kettle hissed on the stove. Her fingers wrapped around a chipped mug, its warmth seeping into her skin. She hadn't yet written the reply—the one that would tell them she wasn't coming home, not next spring, not at all. Not because she was lost, but because she had found something here that felt, at last, like belonging.

The knock came abruptly—three brisk raps against the wood. Brutus sprang to attention with a growl, then a bark. She rose, heart fluttering. No one visited unannounced on Christmas Day.

When she opened the door, the cold struck first—sharp and clean, a blade against the skin. And then: Frank. Snow dusted his coat, a prairie chicken hung from one gloved hand, a canvas sack in the other.

"Merry Christmas," he said, his grin boyish beneath the brim of his cap.

She laughed, breath visible between them. "You're mad. Come in."

He stepped inside, stamping snow from his boots. Brutus greeted him with unabashed joy, tail thumping. He leaned down to ruffle the dog's ears, his gaze flicking toward her.

"Thought I'd bring you dinner. Prairie chicken's not much, but it beats biscuits."

"It's perfect," she said, the words steadier than she felt. Her solitude had been a fortress, carefully assembled. He'd walked through it without a knock.

As she set a pot to boil, he shrugged off his coat, laying the sack beside the hearth. The contents—potatoes, carrots, a tin of cranberry preserve—seemed almost miraculous.

"I'm not intruding?" he asked after a beat, his voice softer now, wary.

"No," she said. "You're exactly what this house needed. It just didn't know it yet."

They worked in tandem, peeling and chopping, their hands brushing now and then like notes in an unfinished chord. The warmth between them grew not from the fire, but from the silence they shared without strain.

"You're sure I'm not ruining some sacred tradition?" He asked, rinsing potatoes in the basin.

"Please," she said, grinning. "I've never made a Christmas meal in my life. Back home, we had a cook who started preparations in October. My greatest contribution was opening the sherry."

"And now you're roasting prairie chicken over a wood stove."

"With a man who shows up uninvited," she teased, nudging him lightly with her hip.

"Uninvited?"

"Uninvited," she echoed, softer now. "But not unwelcome."

"I kept thinking about you," he said at last, eyes on the blade in his hand. "Out here alone, your first Christmas away."

She paused, setting down the peeler. "I was bracing for it. But you... shifted something."

He glanced at her, and something unspoken passed between them, a recognition, quiet but absolute. She turned back to her work, her heart moving too fast to measure.

Later, after the meal—roasted bird, vegetables glistening with butter, a table cobbled together with gratitude—they sat before the stove. Frank uncorked a flask.

"Brandy," he said. "A gift from a trapper. Not mine to hoard."

She sipped, coughed, laughed. "It's like swallowing firelight."

He pulled something from his coat pocket, wrapped in brown paper and twine. "For you."

She unwrapped it carefully: moccasins, hand-stitched, lined with fur. She slipped them on, and warmth bloomed up her calves.

"These floors are cold," he said.

"And you thought of that," she said, not meaning the floor at all.

Their eyes lingered. The space between them hummed with something newly known, too fragile to name.

"Come on," he said. "Let's try them out."

Wrapped in blankets, tucked in the toboggan, they rode to the ridge above the cabin. The sky, bruised with stars, unfolded above them. The Northern Lights unfurled in long ribbons—green, violet, the faintest shimmer of blue—like brushstrokes across night.

The dogs circled close. Brutus nestled behind them like a warm stone.

They didn't speak. They didn't need to.

She leaned into him, shoulder against his chest, and let her breath fall into the same rhythm as his.

The sky writhed and danced, and beneath it, they stayed still—two people suspended in a quiet too profound for loneliness.

She tilted her head back, eyes reflecting the aurora. "You know," she said, voice nearly lost in the hush, "this might be the best Christmas I've ever had."

Frank turned to her, eyebrows lifting.

"And I've had some very fine ones," she added, "with linens and music and enough candles to burn down the house."

He smiled. "What's different?"

She paused. "This one is real."

In the hush of that prairie Christmas, wrapped in fur and silence, Mary didn't just see the North. She felt it claim her, completely.

And this time, she didn't resist.

CHAPTER 51

The awakening prairie lay sprawling under the bright March sky, its vast expanse unfurling with the promise of spring. Mary, a healer now almost a year in these northern lands, stood outside her humble home. The sun, generous and warm, poured its rays over her, chasing away the last whispers of winter. She busied herself with collecting firewood, sleeves rolled, breath clouding softly in the chill.

In the distance, the clip-clop of hooves cut through the stillness. Her heart stirred at the sound—familiar, comforting. She turned, eyes scanning the trail.

"There he is," she said aloud, smiling wide. Brutus's ears perked before he bolted forward, barking with joy.

A neighboring farmer came into view, reins in hand, leading another horse—Danny, her companion and steadfast partner in healing. His coat gleamed in the sun, and as he caught sight of her, his pace quickened.

Brutus circled them, tail wagging madly, while she stepped forward, laughter escaping her lips. "Danny, my boy, you're back!"

He nuzzled into her shoulder, breath warm against her collarbone. She pulled a handful of carrots from her pocket. "I bet you've missed these."

As he crunched them down, she stroked his mane, feeling again that unspoken understanding between them. Brutus, ever enthusiastic, grabbed the reins in his mouth and tugged.

"Easy there," she said, laughing. "We've got work to do—but yes, I missed you too."

She turned to the farmer. "Thank you—for bringing him, and for the message."

The man gave a nod, brushing his gloves together. "She's in a bad way, from what the boy said. Polish family. He came riding just after dawn."

Her expression shifted, her tone settling. "Then we'd best not lose time."

She changed swiftly into her riding clothes. Emerging with her medical bags, she secured them to Danny's saddle and swung up onto his back with practiced ease. Brutus trotted alongside as they headed out, hooves steady on the muddy, thawing trail.

They reached the shack by early afternoon. It stood crooked on uneven ground, its timber dark with age and snowmelt. Smoke curled from a bent stovepipe. Outside, a rusted washtub steamed; inside, the sounds of labor filtered faintly through the walls.

She dismounted and tied Danny to a post. "Wait here, old friend," she murmured. "You've done your part."

Brutus flanked her as she stepped into the one-room home—and was hit with a wall of scent and sound. The place smelled like a barn: straw, manure, smoke, and boiling water. Chickens strutted across the dirt floor. A piglet snorted from beneath a bench. The air shimmered with heat and tension.

Her patient lay on a low cot, face slick with sweat, eyes closed. A teenage boy stood nearby, worry etched deep into his young features.

Mary set her bag down, gently. "Ask her how long she's been in labor."

The boy stammered in Polish. "Since yesterday."

She approached the cot, knelt beside the woman. Her practiced hands moved gently over the woman's belly. She frowned.

"She's breech," she said quietly. A flicker of thought sparked behind her calm expression—*Not here, not now*. But she didn't flinch. She couldn't afford to.

She looked at the boy. "Tell her she must stay calm. The baby's turned wrong. I'll do what I can."

He nodded, translating in halting Polish. The mother's

eyes met hers. Fear, yes—but something else too. A quiet, desperate trust.

Mary's fingers found their place. "We need to turn the baby gently," she murmured, more to herself than anyone else. She focused, hands steady, mind anchored.

The shack buzzed with tension—the hiss of boiling water, the rustle of feathers, the labored breathing of a woman bringing life through pain. She worked with quiet determination, guiding, coaxing. She had done this before. But never here. Never in a place more manger than room, more stable than home.

But she had long stopped expecting clean linens and polished floors. The prairie had taught her that life didn't wait for comfort. It demanded presence. It demanded nerve.

"Keep her calm," she said again. "Tell her the baby is turning. We're almost there."

And then—a shift. Subtle, but sure. Relief surged through her limbs, but she didn't exhale yet.

The baby crowned. Her hands stayed steady, coaxing gently. She watched the woman breathe, her body arching with the force of something ancient and holy.

Then a cry—weak at first, then stronger. A boy. Alive. His mother's face crumpled into sobs. His father leaned in, hands trembling, overcome.

Mary looked up at him. The man's face was a flood of disbelief and awe, eyes glassy as they swept from his newborn to his wife. He opened his mouth, then closed it again, as if no language could meet the weight of what had just passed.

The boy translated her words: "He's going to be fine."

Mary cleaned and swaddled the child, wrapping him in a worn wool blanket. Around them, the shack was transformed—still rustic, still loud with livestock—but now a sanctuary.

Outside, she drew in the clean breath of March, sharp with melt and waking soil. The sun dazzled on patches of melting snow. She patted Danny's neck. Brutus leapt and barked in celebration.

She mounted again, the weight of her bags somehow lighter.

The father and son stood at the door, their waves silent but full.

And as she rode back across the awakening land, Mary Percy—doctor, daughter, stranger-turned-healer—felt her purpose settle in her chest like a second heartbeat. Nothing surprised her anymore, not really.

Even miracles felt like part of the job.

CHAPTER 52

Mary found herself in the embrace of spring at her humble home. The almost-finished barn stood testament to the hard work she had poured into her homestead. In the paddock, she brushed down Danny, his coat glossy under the warming sun. The prairie shimmered with promise.

In the distance, an engine's low hum broke the quiet. A car jostled down the trail, wheels kicking up dust. She squinted. Then, a wave from the driver—Frank. Brutus launched forward, tail high, barking with delight.

She laid down the brush and walked to the paddock fence where Frank had stopped. The Chevrolet looked like it had survived a minor war.

"Why, hello, Frank. What do you have there?"

"Just came up from Peace River," he said, grinning. "Bought myself a '27 Chevrolet. What do you think?"

She sized it up. "Can it jump logs and ford rivers?"

His laugh broke easily. "Not yet. But it'll get us to town faster than Danny. And it's perfect weather for a picnic."

She looked at Danny, brushing her hand down his neck. "What do you think, boy? Should I betray you for four wheels and a sputtering engine?"

Danny blinked slowly. Brutus barked like he'd already packed the sandwiches.

She told him to stay behind and watch things. Brutus whined but obeyed, settling with a dramatic sigh.

They drove to a riverbank where the valley opened wide. Blankets laid out, sandwiches unwrapped, lemonade poured. The air carried the scent of damp earth and opening buds.

"That was lovely," she said later, brushing crumbs from her skirt.

"The pleasure was mine. I had some business in town. The car was just part of it," he said casually, though something in his tone gave him away.

She leaned back on her elbows. "The roads are half mud and the other half potholes. You planning to float this thing home like a canoe?"

"It won't make it up to Keg River yet," he admitted with a grin. "I was thinking of keeping it here. With you. If that's alright."

Her brows lifted. "You mean for me to use?"

He nodded. "You ride Danny ten, sometimes fifty miles a day. I figured maybe the both of you deserve a break."

She laughed. "A break? Frank, unless your Chevrolet can leap a fence, cross a flooded creek, and trot through the bush, I'm not sure she's up to the job."

He chuckled. "I just thought—on dry days, for the easier runs... maybe you wouldn't mind having the option."

She tilted her head, mock serious. "So this isn't an elaborate ploy to see me again under the guise of tire maintenance?"

"Might be a bit of both."

She paused, looking out over the sunlit valley. "Well... I suppose if it can make it to Mrs. Sandor's without rattling apart, it might earn its keep."

He smiled. "So... deal?"

She extended her hand, still teasing. "Only if it comes with driving lessons. I don't want to end up in a ditch before spring."

He took her hand gently. "Deal."

They sipped more lemonade, and the conversation turned.

"Your government contract's nearly up," he said. "Any thoughts on what's next?"

She nodded, a glimmer in her eyes. "I wrote to the Minister of Health. Told him I'd stay if they'd have me—serving homesteaders and the natives."

"So you're staying?"

Her answer came bright. "Frank, I've never felt so alive. This land—it's in my bones now. I couldn't possibly return to England."

He tried to mask it, but his smile gave him away. She went on, gentle but firm. "Here by the river—with Danny, Brutus, my garden, my patients—it's not just a place anymore. It's home. I'm even thinking of buying a homestead."

His face dimmed. "Buy land here? Mary, this isn't farming country. Just gravel ridges and scrub. Not worth five hundred dollars."

"Frank," she said softly, "I'm not looking to farm. I want a home."

He rubbed his jaw. "Alright. Just don't want you throwing money into the muskeg."

"I'm not rushing anything," she said. "But if I'm going to stay, I'll need roots."

He quieted, hands fidgeting with the empty flask. Then: "There's something I need to say."

She paused, sensing the shift. "Alright."

"These past months... they've meant more to me than I've said. The idea of you setting up a life without me—"

She turned to him, her expression open.

"It's not jealousy," he said quickly. "It's just... you matter to me. More than I ever expected."

She reached for his hand. "Frank, I care for you too. But I've also found something else here—myself."

"Yourself?"

She smiled. "In England, doctors hang a brass plate outside their offices. A symbol of permanence. Belonging. I used to imagine mine. But I never felt it—until now. Until here."

He nodded slowly, something settling in his eyes. "Then hang it here."

Their kiss came not as surprise, but as inevitability. A sealing of hearts already halfway joined.

Later, as the car rumbled back toward her home, Brutus bounded into view. The sun, low on the horizon, cast long shadows across the barn.

"I have to go," he said, regretful.

"I wish you didn't."

"I'll be back in June. To take furs to Edmonton."

"I know I can wait," she said. "I just don't want to."

"Neither do I."

One last kiss. One last look.

He drove off, dust in his wake. She stood with Brutus, hand resting on his head, heart brimming with promise.

In the quiet that followed, the prairie whispered its approval.

And Mary knew: this wasn't the end of something.

It was the beginning.

CHAPTER 53

The morning light bathed her home in a serene glow, the golden rays filtering through the weathered screens and casting soft patterns across the worn floorboards. Mary moved with quiet rhythm through her chores, each motion a kind of meditation—splitting kindling, wiping down the table, placing a pot to boil for tea. Her solitude was rarely disturbed, and she had grown fond of its cadence.

So when the knock came—a firm, precise rap—it drew her still.

She turned, drying her hands on her apron, and moved to the door. Standing at her screen was Constable Lucerne, upright and composed in his RCMP uniform, his cap held respectfully in his hand. The man carried an air of practiced gravity, but something in his eyes made her pulse lift.

She offered a steady smile. "Morning, Constable. What brings you to my doorstep today?"

"Good morning, Doctor," he said, his French accent shaping each word with crisp precision. "I'm afraid this is no social call. I need your expertise."

"Please, come in. Have a seat."

She motioned to the chair by the table. He stepped inside, removing his coat as he did. She noted the stiffness in his posture—not formal, but burdened.

"Since your government contract was renewed," he began, "you also serve as coroner in this district, yes?"

She nodded. "That's correct."

He paused just long enough to let the implication settle. "There's been a death at Keg River. A man. We're investigating a possible murder."

The word murder didn't belong here—not in this land of long silences and harder lives. Mary blinked, as if trying to place the word in the right context, but it wouldn't sit still.

"A murder?" she echoed, the disbelief threading through her voice. "Up here?"

He nodded, expression unreadable. "That's what we need to find out."

She set her teacup down, the china clinking gently on wood. Already recalibrating her day. "When do we leave?"

"Tomorrow at dawn," he stated with precise clarity.

After he left, she stood for a moment at the screen door, watching his figure disappear down the trail. The light still fell golden and gentle, but the air had shifted—no longer the soft stillness of morning, but the taut, expectant quiet before a storm. She turned back to her tasks, hands moving, mind already gathering what she'd need.

Dawn broke cold and bright. Frost glittered on the grass as she climbed into Lucerne's truck, her satchel of instruments at her feet. They rode in silence, the road winding north past melting drifts and thaw-softened fields.

As they crested a rise, Keg River came into view— modest buildings hugged by woodland and open sky. Frank's trading post stood solid and square, smoke curling from the chimney.

Lucerne pulled the truck to a stop in front of the trading post.

Frank stepped out, brushing sawdust from his sleeves. When his eyes met Mary's, surprise flickered—then settled into something warmer. His smile reached her in full.

"Morning," he said, approaching the truck. "Didn't expect to see you today."

"Nor I you," she replied, stepping down onto the

gravel. The smell of fresh-cut wood and pipe smoke hung in the cool air.

Lucerne exchanged a few clipped words with Frank in fluent French—efficient, familiar. Mary caught only fragments, but it was clear: this wasn't their first collaboration.

Then Lucerne turned to her. "I asked Mr. Jackson to join us. He knows the MacMillan family—and the terrain out there's tricky. Could be helpful."

She looked at Frank, whose expression held quiet resolve.

She nodded. "Of course. That makes sense."

Frank gave her a small, reassuring smile. "I'll follow in my truck. I know the back road—cuts off a good fifteen minutes."

She climbed back into the cab beside Lucerne. As they pulled away from the post, she cast a glance in the side mirror—Frank was already behind the wheel, starting the engine.

She didn't say it aloud, but she was grateful. Whatever lay ahead, she wouldn't be facing it alone.

They drove out past the edges of town, where the landscape grew more ragged, dotted with larch and scrub pine. The MacMillan farm emerged as a hushed ruin of hope. The fields lay unseeded, wind stirring dry tufts of last year's grass. The shack stood lopsided and gray, porch boards sagging, windows patched with rags.

Lucerne parked, and they stepped out.

The front door creaked open under Lucerne's hand. Inside, the air was stale with old smoke and something heavier—grief, regret, the ache of endings. She set her bag down near the cold stove.

A body lay on the floor, motionless. Face turned away. Nothing moved, not even the air.

Lucerne spoke quietly. "The Trosky boy found him two nights ago. Reported it yesterday morning. No sign of struggle. No weapon in sight."

Mary knelt beside the body, her movements careful. She checked the hands, the position of the limbs, the discoloration. Then, at the collarbone, she noticed residue—fine, dark, and unmistakable.

"Gunpowder," she said softly. "Close range."

Lucerne frowned. "So… suicide?"

"Could be. But the weapon's missing."

Frank stepped inside now, scanning the room. "He was a solitary man. Jim Bank. Didn't say much. Kept to himself."

Lucerne nodded. "That fits. But we need more."

Mary moved toward the far corner, her eyes scanning

the floorboards beneath the rickety furniture. A dull glint caught her eye under a broken chair leg. She crouched slowly.

"There," she said, pointing. "A revolver."

Lucerne stepped forward, reaching into his coat pocket. He pulled out a pair of black gloves and tugged them on with a snap. Crouching beside her, he retrieved the weapon carefully, turning it in his gloved hands.

"Recently fired," he murmured. He opened the chamber. "One spent cartridge. Five still loaded."

Mary stood, arms crossed. "If it was suicide... wouldn't there be a note?"

Frank, who had been quietly surveying the room, turned toward the desk. His hands moved lightly over scattered papers, sifting through receipts and dog-eared invoices.

"Nothing here," he said, brow furrowed.

Then he paused, narrowing his eyes. A piece of paper lay curled near the stove, barely visible in the shadows. Wind, or a boot, must've shifted it.

He stepped closer, bent to retrieve it, and unfolded the page. His voice was low.

"It's a letter. Not addressed. Looks like a confession."

Lucerne took the paper from him and read it silently,

his expression unreadable at first. Then he nodded slowly.

"Yes. This explains it. He intended this. It's written clearly."

Mary exhaled. Her features remained composed, but the room seemed to close in around them. A silence fell, not out of confusion, but grief. She let it linger a moment, before speaking.

Lucerne handed her the letter, then looked at the revolver again. "Your assessment, Doctor Percy, confirms the timeline. The residue, the wound, the confession—all consistent."

He stood, removing the gloves carefully. "I'll log the evidence."

Mary rose slowly, brushing the dust from her coat. "I'll get him ready. Can you bring the stretcher in?"

Frank nodded and returned with Lucerne, the two men moving carefully as she oversaw each step. She worked in quiet concentration—cleaning, securing, noting details for the report. Death demanded dignity, even in a place like this.

When the stretcher was secured in the back of the constable's truck, Lucerne closed the doors with a quiet finality.

He turned to her. "I'll take him to Peace River. No need for you to ride back—I've got it from here."

Mary nodded. "Thank you, Constable."

Lucerne tipped his hat. "Merci encore, docteur. Good work today."

She turned to Frank, her voice softer. "Think you could get me home?"

Frank gave a small smile. "Wouldn't have it any other way."

She gave a small nod, then turned toward Frank's truck, the dust already beginning to settle behind Lucerne's as he drove off.

Once they were inside and the engine started, the silence wrapped around them again—familiar, not uncomfortable. They bumped down the rutted trail, the weight of the morning still pressing gently between them.

"Are you alright?" Frank asked as they reached the turnoff toward the river.

She looked ahead, then down at her hands. "It's always strange, being so close to the end of someone's story. Especially when no one else saw it coming."

He nodded. "There's a lot of that up here. Isolation eats at people."

She glanced at him. "But connection can save them. Sometimes even a kind word makes a difference."

He didn't reply, just reached across and gave her hand a squeeze.

Later, they pulled up to Frank's homestead. The air had warmed slightly. The wind moved gently through the trees.

"I appreciate you letting me stay tonight," she said quietly. "I don't think I could be alone after that."

"You're not alone," he said simply.

She smiled, a soft one that reached her eyes. A pause held between them—full of quiet understanding.

Together, they stepped inside, the door closing behind them. Outside, the prairie kept its peace, bearing witness to all that passed—and all that remained.

She reached for his hand—and this time, he didn't let go. Not now. Not again.

CHAPTER 54

Frank led her into his log home, a sanctuary carved from the very marrow of the northern woods. The walls, thick with time and timber, exhaled the quiet strength of spruce and cedar. A stone hearth anchored the room, its embers casting soft flickers across the grain of handcrafted furniture. Everything spoke of Frank—his hands, his patience, his solitude made visible in wood and iron.

Mary stood still, letting the quiet settle into her. The place was more than shelter. It was presence. History. A lived-in poem carved by calloused hands.

"Frank, this is beautiful," she said softly. Her fingers traced the back of a chair, its joints smoothed by use. "Did you make all this yourself?"

He gave a modest nod, his voice touched with understated pride. "I try to make what I need. Helps to stay busy."

Her eyes moved over the walls, noting the simple

art—a charcoal drawing of a riverbend, an old map pinned with brass tacks, a small wooden carving of a fox. Light poured through the south-facing window, laying a golden wash over the room.

"And this?" she asked, gesturing to a carved table leg, delicate as antlers.

"Yes," he said again, a smile playing at the corner of his mouth.

She was about to ask more when his arms came around her from behind. The gesture caught her off guard, but it felt right—solid, steady. She leaned into him, the long breath she hadn't known she was holding slipping out at last.

"Frank," she murmured, "these past days... birth, death, everything in between... it makes all of this," she glanced around, then back at him, "feel even more precious."

His lips brushed her cheek. "It's all part of it, Mary. Joy and grief. Sometimes side by side. But it's the sharing of it that keeps us human."

She turned in his arms, facing him fully. "Being here with you... it's like standing still in a storm. Like I can finally breathe."

He held her gaze, eyes warm and sure. "When you're here, the house feels whole. Everything makes sense."

He stepped away, just long enough to retrieve a small,

wrapped bundle from the shelf.

"I was saving this," he said. "But now feels right."

Inside the brown paper, she found a brass nameplate. The lettering was crisp, the engraving deep:

'Dr. Mary Percy Jackson

Office Hours

2:30-4:30 p.m.

Weekdays, and By Appointment'

She stared at it, the words catching in her chest. Her name. Her title. Her purpose.

"My brass plate," she whispered, voice catching. "Like in England."

He nodded. "It belongs on a door. Here. Mine, if you'll have it."

A long pause passed between them, the moment full and unspeakable.

"Frank, are you—?"

He took her hand, grounding her. "Will you marry me?"

The room was still. The fire crackled once, as though

to mark the asking. She looked at him—the lines around his eyes, the steady kindness in his face, the home he had built and offered to share.

"Yes," she said. "Yes, I will."

Their embrace, quiet and certain, sealed something already written between them. In that room of wood and firelight, a life came into focus. Not perfect, not easy—but real. Shared.

She kissed him, and he kissed her back, and the prairie wind moved against the windows, bearing witness. The scent of pine. The slow warmth of the fire. The brass plate heavy in her hands—all of it, a promise.

DJ ATKINSON

BATTLE RIVER PRAIRIE

A Journey of the Heart

DJ ATKINSON

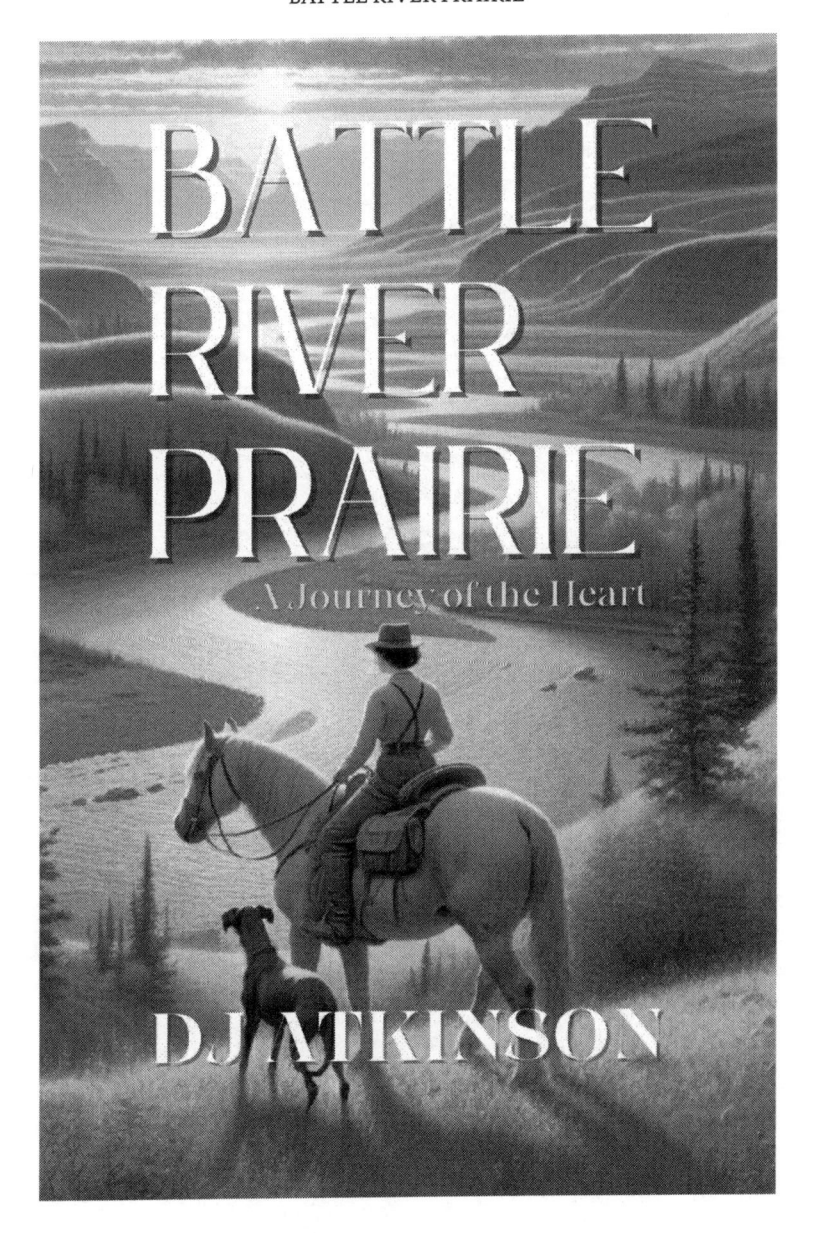

About the Author

DJ Atkinson is a debut novelist based on Protection Island, British Columbia. After a long career in real estate and mortgage lending, he turned his focus toward fiction, drawn to quiet stories of endurance, belonging, and place. Battle River Prairie is his first novel—a deeply researched and lyrically written account of Dr. Mary Percy Jackson, one of Alberta's first female frontier physicians.

DJ first discovered Mary through a friend whose great-grandmother she was. That personal connection led him to archived materials, family anecdotes, and historical accounts. What emerged was not only the story of a remarkable doctor but a portrait of character: someone resourceful, kind, and quietly radical in her time.

Set over the course of a single year, Battle River Prairie follows Mary's arrival in Northern Alberta in the 1920s, where she serves a vast territory by dog sled, horseback, and canoe. The novel captures her evolving relationship with the land, with her patients—pioneer farmers, immigrants, and Indigenous families—and with herself. Rather than dramatizing her heroism, the book reveals it in subtle acts: a birth safely navigated, a hard ride answered, a moment of stillness earned.

DJ is currently working on the next novel in the series, continuing Mary's extraordinary journey across the North. His goal is to create a literary tribute that honours not only her story but the larger quiet histories of women whose lives helped shape the land we now inherit.

Books by DJ Atkinson

DJ ATKINSON

Manufactured by Amazon.ca
Bolton, ON